HEARTBEAT :

CONSTABLE IN DISGUISE

Nicholas Rhea

This edition first
published by Accent Press Ltd – 2009

ISBN 9781906373429

First Published in Hardback by
Robert Hale Ltd 1989

Printed and bound in the UK

Cover Design by Red Dot Design

About The Author

Nicholas Rhea is the pen-name of Peter N. Walker, formerly an inspector with the North Yorkshire Police and the creator of the *Constable* series of books from which the Yorkshire TV series *Heartbeat* has been derived.

Nicholas Rhea tells of some of the colourful incidents and eccentric Yorkshire characters encountered by a country constable, stories which provided the basis for the adventures of PC Nick Rowan, played by Nick Berry, in the TV series.

Peter N. Walker is also the author of *Portrait of the North York Moors* and, married with four children, lives in North Yorkshire.

Chapter 1

Detection is, or ought to be, an exact science, and should be treated in the same cold and unemotional manner.

SIR ARTHUR CONAN DOYLE (1859-1930)

IN THE LARGE AND uncertain world outside the police service, the letters CID are widely assumed to mean 'Criminal Investigation Department'. In the minds of countless citizens, particularly those approaching the autumn of their years, these initials conjure up near-romantic images of trilby-hatted men in overlarge raincoats who go about mysterious work which is far too important and intellectual to be trusted to uniformed police officers.

Most of us possess a mental picture of a typical detective but there is no modern requirement for them to wear trilbies or belted raincoats. Indeed, the ideal detective should look nothing like a police officer. Too many bygone sleuths looked too much like off-duty police officers, with their short haircuts, big polished shoes, trilby hats and belted raincoats – they wore what was in effect a civilian uniform, which often defeated the purpose of wearing plain clothes. Happily, many of today's detectives do not look like police officers in their designer jeans, trainer shoes and expensive casual wear.

And this is where the real meaning of CID ought to be mentioned – it means 'Constable in Disguise'.

1

Constables in Disguise, or detectives as they are better known, are usually depicted entering or leaving the mighty portals of the original Scotland Yard which stood on the banks of the River Thames in London, England, in the manner of some legendary and impenetrable castle. Associated with this image are black Wolseley police cars, Black Marias, turned-up raincoat collars, loosened belts, short haircuts, magnifying glasses and the habit of addressing all other male persons as 'sir', particularly those under investigation. The number of 'sirs' emitted during an interview varies proportionately with the importance of the interview or the social class of the interviewee.

An adjunct to this perpetual image of Scotland Yard's famous detectives was the notion that all really serious crime in the United Kingdom was solved by them and that the bumpkins in the shire forces were fit only for riding bikes in pursuit of poachers or telling the time.

It is surprising how many Americans and other foreigners, and indeed what a high level of British folk, still think that Scotland Yard investigates every British murder or indeed every British crime. This is a myth, of course, but it has been fostered by many past crime writers who have dramatised Scotland Yard departments like the Flying Squad, the Murder Squad and the Fraud Squad. Their heroic members swooped around Britain keeping the streets free from villainy.

Those detectives never walked anywhere, nor did they proceed, travel, gallop or simply move. They always swooped, or so it seemed from contemporary novels and newspaper reports. The outcome of this PR exercise was that many authors, and thus many of their readers, constantly failed to appreciate that the provincial police forces had, and still have, some very good detectives. The truth is that all provincial criminal investigation departments are very capable of solving their own crimes. Indeed, there seems no reason why the Yard should not call them in to solve a few of London's trickier cases.

Another oft-repeated myth perpetuated by some crime writers is that all murders are committed either on express trains or in the libraries of country houses during dinner. Followers of this mythology may also believe that dead bodies do not mess the carpets or smell after an hour or so of lying around the house. In fact, dead bodies are not very nice things. The truth is they are terribly cumbersome and something of a problem to deal with, a fact known to most police officers. Furthermore, dead bodies that have been subjected to the inhuman treatment dished out by some murderers and rapists are very nasty, messy and smelly indeed. Furthermore, criminals of all types are not very nice people, in spite of what some sociologists would have us believe. They are so often the dregs of society who are able to masquerade as decent folk until the police are able to prove otherwise.

It follows that it takes a rather special person to become a successful detective. That person must have intelligence, which is not necessarily the same as intellectual ability; he or she must also have a deep working knowledge of criminal law and the legal procedures involved in the prosecution of criminals, as well as an immense understanding of people and their behavioural traits, plus, of course, a keen eye for detail, good powers of observation, a very alert and enquiring mind and infinite patience. The latter quality is needed to cope with those long moments of drudgery and the wealth of interminable, plodding and fruitless enquiries.

It might be prudent to mention here that police

officers are not necessarily promoted when they join the CID. They are often transferred to plain clothes duties without promotion to a higher rank; an officer may be a police constable (PC) one day and a detective police constable (D/PC) – abbreviated to Detective Constable (D/C) – the next. Such a move is not a promotion, because the detective remains in the rank of constable – it is a sideways transfer. But a detective constable *can* be promoted either to a uniform sergeant (Sgt), or to a detective sergeant (D/S). Within the ranks of the CID, there is detective sergeant, detective inspector (D/I), detective chief inspector (D/C/I), detective superintendent (D/Supt) and detective chief superintendent (D/Chief Supt).

All police officers begin their careers in uniform, but there can be promotion right through the ranks of the CID or, alternatively, elevation to the senior heights of the service is sometimes gained by switching from uniform to CID and back again as the opportunities arise. Young constables often join the police service having read books about the great detectives or even about Sherlock Holmes, Hercule Poirot *et al*; their desire is sometimes to become a famous sleuth, albeit within the ranks of the police service and not as a private investigator. So they opt for at least two years plodding the beat in uniform before being eligible to further their careers as members of the elite CID.

But becoming a detective is not easy.

It requires the initial ability to make known one's skills to those who select recruits for the CID, and in my young constabulary days selection was followed (or occasionally preceded) by a thirteen-week intensive Detective Training Course. This included criminal law, legal procedures and methods of detection, in the form of lectures, and practical work on fingerprints, forensic science, scientific aids, the administration of a murder investigation or serious crime inquiry, identification methods and that host of worldly necessities that makes a good CID officer.

There was the TIC procedure to understand too.

This can be somewhat complicated, but in simple terms it is where an arrested person confesses to the police that he or she has committed other crimes which have not, up to that stage, been prosecuted or even detected. When an arrested person is charged with a crime, therefore, he or she is questioned about other undetected crimes of a similar nature for which he or she may be responsible. If the arrested person admits any further crimes, they are added to the charge sheet and presented to the court as admissions of guilt. When determining the cases, the court will 'take into consideration' those other confessed crimes, although a case of careless driving would not be dealt with at the same time as fifteen burglary charges. The crimes which are TIC'd must be similar in nature to each other. The chances are that the villain will receive a sentence lighter than if his list of crimes had been detected and presented to a court individually. Thus the TIC system is beneficial to convicted criminals because it allows them to wipe clean their proverbial slate and, when they are released, to start committing a whole range of new crimes.

This system is also useful to the police. It means that strings of crimes can often be written off as 'detected,' a pleasing state of affairs when submitting returns for publication in the Home Office's annual *Criminal Statistics for England and Wales*. A good example would occur where a burglar is arrested, his house is searched and a veritable Aladdin's Cave of stolen goods is discovered. Those objects are the loot from several earlier crimes. He then admits breaking into other premises from which he stole those items. If the arrested person agrees, those other crimes would, in police jargon, be TIC'd 'taken into consideration' by the court when passing sentence.

Another important thing to learn was when, or when not, to 'crime' a complaint. If a complaint is 'crimed', it means that the investigating officer is satisfied that indeed a crime has been committed. For example, lots of women rush into police stations on Saturday afternoons to complain that their handbags have been stolen or that their purses have been stolen from the top of their shopping bags. In truth, how many of these are really lost or mislaid? The answer is: quite a lot! So if a detective is informed by a woman that her handbag has been stolen, he will first make sure that she has not mislaid it. This is not an easy assessment to make but it is one that must be done.

It is a fact that people do feel they are the victims of crime when a loss is either their own fault or a misunderstanding of some kind. I knew a dear lady pensioner who was convinced someone was stealing her coal, whereas she was simply using it faster than she thought. I knew a man who complained that his garden spade had been stolen, whereas he had lent it to a friend and had forgotten about the loan until he wanted to dig his garden six months later. I knew a woman who left her handbag on a park bench. She realised she'd left it behind and returned within minutes, but it was missing upon her return, so she reported it stolen. In those few moments, it had in fact been found and handed in to the park authorities by an honest finder.

There are thousands of such losses every day. If every

lost item was 'crimed', the crime rate would soar and the detection rate would slump. So crimes are recorded as such only when the police are sure they are genuine crimes; hence they are *crimed.*

Bearing in mind the hard work that is needed to become a fully fledged detective, I felt I would like to know more about this branch of police work. I had read my Sherlock Holmes books, I had puzzled over the loopholes in Agatha Christie's efforts, I had seen films about the work of the master detectives and I warmed to the notion of dramatic battles in court when I could prove, by clever reasoning, that my arrested person was guilty of the crime I had alleged. But was it wise for a rural constable to join those whose work deals almost entirely with crime and criminals? Could this jaundice my view of the great British public whom I had sworn to serve? Would I still regard every human being as someone basically decent and honest?

And besides, how does a uniformed village constable break into those hallowed ranks?

In my time, the mid-1960s, the answer lay in a system known as 'Aide to CID' which was an officer's short-term attachment to the Criminal Investigation Department. It involved a six-month period of work with the CID, during which time one's efforts were assessed to see if one was capable of becoming a full-time CID officer. An aptitude for the work would be rewarded by that thirteen-week course at a convenient Detective Training School.

The snag with a North Yorkshire moorland village like Aidensfield was that very little crime was committed and so it was not easy to show one's potential for this specialised work. Another factor was that the crime figures that I had to submit quarterly to my

7

superiors were open to wide interpretation. If I recorded a meagre annual total of twelve crimes upon my beat, the official attitude was that there was no need for a constable to live and work in Aidensfield, as the crime rate was far too low to justify his presence.

Besides, the crimes themselves were at the lower end of the scale of seriousness. For example, some of those crimes might involve little more than the theft of a gallon of petrol from a car (or a crime wave of twelve thefts from twelve cars), or the theft of poultry or sheep, shoplifting from the village stores or the work of a sneak thief in the local council estate who prowls about stealing radios or cash from houses whose doors have been left open while the ladies gossip or drink tea. It was hardly serious crime or Holmesian stuff, and it was not likely to worry the senior officers of the force. However, it was highly upsetting to the victims and to the general morale and well-being of a small community.

But *my* interpretation of such figures was that I was out and about on my beat, keeping down the volume of crime. I claimed that a low rate of crime indicated some very positive policing. In my view, it showed I was doing a good job and that my presence as a resident constable was necessary to keep it that way. I said, and I maintain, that the village constable was and still is an asset to the community. After all, crime prevention is a very sophisticated art, and much of it is achieved by the presence of a patrolling constable in uniform who has the time and the will to stop and chat to his public. Those chats could reveal villains and they could produce crime-prevention advice for those who are less aware of such risks. In addition, the sight of a local constable going about his daily routine does provide a feeling of security within the community.

In several discussions with senior officers about the merits of a resident village constable, I suggested that a high crime rate on Aidensfield beat would be proof that I was *not* doing my job, irrespective of any detection percentage. It is worth mentioning here that most crimes on a rural beat were investigated by the resident officer, and not by the CID.

I followed my arguments with the logic that my beat's annual low crime rate was clear evidence of the value of my presence and also proof of my localised crime-beating efforts. The bosses countered this by saying that, if the village constable was taken away from Aidensfield and not replaced, the volume of crime would not show a significant increase. I agreed with this, but *not* for the same reason as the bosses. I knew that, if there was no constable at Aidensfield, many local crimes would never be reported; the villagers would not bother to contact an anonymous and distant police officer, especially by telephone, to report their losses unless it was a very serious matter. As a consequence, the outcome would be a continuing low number of *reported* crime, but another important aspect was that, in the absence of someone handy to whom to report the smaller crimes, the incidence of true crime could be a lot higher. The absence of a convenient constable would mean that more actual crime would be committed but much less would be reported.

I could not make my superiors understand that, for the type of crimes suffered in the villages, the local people would not contact a distant police station. They'd wait until they met the constable to report matters like, 'Oh, Mr Rhea, I thowt I'd better mention this – somebody got into my implement shed and nicked a coil o' rope last week.'

Or I would receive reports like, 'There's somebody about, Mr Rhea; five or six of us have had money taken, milk money we left on our doorsteps on a morning for t'milkman ... only a few pounds ...'

Another example is that someone would tell me, 'Mr Rhea, awd Mrs Barthram's had somebody in her greenhouse, pinching her garden tools. Two trowels and a spade have gone; she doesn't like bothering you, so I thought I'd mention it ...'

Crimes of this kind would never be reported other than to the local constable as he passed by, and although officers might patrol the villages in cars and vans, who would halt a passing police van to complain of the theft of a coil of rope a week earlier, or that someone had stolen a cactus from Dad's greenhouse? Removal of village constables is a fine way of reducing the volume of reported crime, but their absence can never permit the real level of rural crime to be calculated – and the same argument pertains to acts of vandalism, damage and general anti-social behaviour.

It was while entertaining such thoughts and concern about the future of the village constable that I was on patrol in Ashfordly one autumn morning in 1966. I was standing beside a telephone kiosk, making a point there in case the office wished to contact me (even though I had a radio in the van!), when I noticed the rangy figure of Detective Sergeant Gerry Connolly, who was heading towards me with strong, purposeful strides.

He was the man in charge of the CID at Eltering. Ashfordly and Aidensfield were within his area of responsibility. He was a pleasant man in his early forties who sported a mop of thick fair hair over a face that was as pink and fresh as a child's. Clad in brown brogue shoes, a Harris tweed jacket and cavalry twill trousers, he looked every inch a countryman, which indeed he was. He bred golden retrievers and seemed to be friendly with everyone.

Of course, he wore a brown trilby hat. It was similar to those worn by men who resort to racecourses; I have often wondered why so many male racegoers wear brown trilby hats. There is a sea of them at any racecourse, where they are a group-identifying feature, in the form of mass adornment or professional lids. Gerry had one too, and I do know he liked attending the races, whether on duty or off.

Gerry Connolly addressed everyone by their Christian names, even those of higher rank than himself, the only exceptions being the chief constable and the deputy chief constable. I knew that his small staff enjoyed working with him; it comprised Detective Constable Paul Wharton, who played bowls and kept tropical fish, and Detective Constable Ian Shackleton, who liked beer, haddock-and-chips and trout fishing. The trio made a good, effective and popular team.

'Morning, Nick,' he beamed as he came to a halt at my side. 'It's a pleasant day to be patrolling this pretty place.'

'And what brings the might of the sub-divisional CID to Ashfordly?' I asked with interest. 'Have we a crime in town?'

'Not unless you know something I don't,' he returned. 'No, we've been having a few raids on the local Co-ops. A team is breaking in through the back windows of the storerooms and nicking thousands of fags each time. Six or seven Co-ops have been raided in the county since the summer. I've just been for words with your local manager; I've tried to persuade him to have bars fitted to all his back windows and better locks

11

fitted on the doors.'

'We've been telling him that for months,' I said. 'We read about the raids in our circulars, but he seemed to think it could never happen to his shop.'

'I'm going round all those that haven't been hit,' he said. 'I reckon he's got the message now; he says it's a decision which has to be made by higher authority, and they're a bit tight with their budgets for improvements and alterations to premises. They're not too concerned about the thefts because the insurance will cover the losses.'

'The poor old insurance companies, they do fork out for a lot of carelessness, don't they?'

'Some are tightening up their conditions now, Nick; they insist on proper safeguards.'

We chattered awhile about professional matters and personal affairs, and then, quite unexpectedly, he said, 'Look, Nick, you're about due for a spell as an Aide, aren't you?'

'I'd enjoy that,' I said, for it was true.

'Right, leave it with me,' he beamed. 'I'll submit your name. It'll take a few weeks to be processed and considered, but I reckon, if I ask for you, they'll approve.'

I returned home feeling very pleased at this promise and explained to my wife that CID duties would entail long hours albeit with no night shifts. One difference would be that I should be expected to spend my evenings at work, visiting the pubs and clubs in the area to quaff pints with the best and the worst elements of society. I would receive a small detective allowance to help defray such expenses, but it would not cover the actual cost. Mary was happy for me and we both knew that I would enjoy this kind of work.

And so it was that in the early summer of the following year I received a formal note from the superintendent to say that I was to be seconded to the CID at Eltering as an Aide for a period of six months.

On the appointed date, therefore, I dressed in a sports jacket, flannels and comfortable shoes, kissed Mary and our four infants farewell and set out for Eltering. I was due to start work at 9 a.m. that Monday but had no idea when that first day's duties would finish. I would be working some very long days during the next six months.

Mary would have to suffer some extended periods alone with our little family, and for me it would be an expensive time.

I did ponder the moral issues of whether I should be spending necessary cash in the pursuit of villains when, all the time, the growing family needed it. But I came to regard my forthcoming period of high expenditure as an investment, believing that, if I did well in my new task, I might get promoted.

But as I drove to Eltering that morning, I decided I would not spend my money on one certain item – I would not buy a trilby hat.

Chapter 2

The two divinest things this world has got,
A lovely woman in a rural spot!
JAMES HENRY LEIGH HUNT (1784-1859)

MY FIRST MORNING IN the bustling CID office at Eltering Police Station was spent among a pile of old books, because my three new colleagues were each telephoning all over the place, writing reports, interviewing callers and liaising with the uniform duty inspector on current criminal matters within the sub-division. There seemed to be an inordinate amount of frantic activity, but that is often the impression gained when entering the sanctum of another; people always appear to be so busy, and they generally have little time for the newcomer. I simply sat at the end of a desk and observed it all.

I heard them discussing a spate of local motor-car thefts and, of much more interest, a series of confidence tricks on the landlords of local inns.

That latter series was based on the simple premise that we all like to get summat for nowt – in this case, the temptation was oceans of whisky at cut price. It was being offered by the con men for cash in advance, with a free bottle as a symbol of good faith. Those landlords with tied houses were not allowed to sell their own selections of beer or spirits, and so this system offered them a few bottles which they could sell without the brewery's knowledge. This in turn would produce cash sales, so offering the dream of tax-free and accounts-free money for themselves from unauthorised and surreptitious sales. A nice way of earning a bit of pocket money.

As a result, when the trickster called with his offer of whisky at a bargain price, the very favourable terms involving cash in advance, many landlords saw it as a means of earning a quick tax-free profit. They gave cash to the con man, enough to buy several crates, but got one bottle of whisky. They never saw their money again nor any of the other promised bottles. Some had ordered dozens and laid out hundreds of pounds.

Members of the uniform branch were instructed to visit all the local pubs to warn landlords of this ploy, but in some instances their warning was too late. The lure of easy cash had cost them dear.

The three detectives had no time to explain things that morning, and I entertained myself by browsing through old records. Boring as they were, the battered books were of some value. There was a photograph album of local criminals, some of whom must have been dead for at least half a century; it was an ancient volume whose original entries were in splendid copperplate writing and whose contents were a list of MOs of local criminals – an MO being, in criminal jargon, a 'method of operation', from the Latin '*modus operandi*'.

MOs were an important means of identifying the work of a criminal – one local housebreaker, for example, always broke in through rear kitchen windows of the houses he attacked. He always smashed the glass by sticking treacle and brown paper over it, then hit it with a brick. This muffled the noise of the breaking glass and held most of the pieces together so he could quickly and easily dispose of them. We always recognised his method of operation.

A more modern book contained details of those awful tricksters who wheedled cash out of pensioners and simple folk by their smooth-tongued lies. In North Yorkshire, the dialect term for such evil operators is 'slape-tongued varmints' – 'slippery-tongued vermin'. 'Slape' is a dialect word for 'slippery', and there are 'slape-faced 'uns' too (people with untrustworthy faces).

So far as the slape-tongued varmints were concerned, it was the laying or repairing of drives to houses and farms and the repairing of roofs which were a popular form of deception at that time. It worked like this – a team of rogues would arrive unannounced and offer to tarmac a drive to a house or farm and then charge an abortive sum for their shoddy work. Another device was to inform pensioners that, while driving past their home, they had noticed that the chimney-stack was on the point of collapse or that a hole had developed in the roof. Having thus alarmed the old folks, the villains offered to repair it immediately out of the kindness of their hearts (!). They would then ask for cash in advance, 'to buy the materials', or they would fix the defect (which often did not exist) for a fee which was well above normal.

They would either disappear with the advanced cash or do the job and then terrify the pensioners into paying a ridiculously high fee. Every one of us wanted to catch these scoundrels, and so those accounts of their trickery were very closely studied. A lot of these villains came from Leeds, and so the crimes became known as the work of 'the Leeds Repairers'.

Sadly, in most cases, it was difficult getting a clear story or a description of the varmints from the pensioners. Even if we did get a coherent story and identified the slape-tongued varmints, it was difficult proving they had committed a crime rather than an act which was merely an unsatisfactory business transaction. There were many times when their activities did not come within the province of the police or the scope of the criminal law. It often depended upon the precise wording they used at the time of committing their evil deeds. Hoping to arrest some of them or their ilk, I swotted up lists of outstanding crimes, some going back ten or twelve years without being solved.

I was then shown the finer points of compiling a crime report and how to complete the necessary statistical forms that accompanied such a report. It was all very baffling, and there seemed to be so much paperwork to complete, but I knew it would all become clearer when I had to record my first real crime as an Aide. And that baptism occurred that very same afternoon.

It was three o'clock and I was in the office with D/PC Ian Shackleton. He was explaining the problems of investigating the crime of shop-breaking. He was highlighting the fact that some shop-owners or their managers claimed that items had been stolen because they needed to cover up deficiencies in the stock which were of their own making, through either carelessness or dishonesty. There were some who set fire to their premises in order to claim from their insurance companies, and I was rapidly realizing that genuinely honest people seemed to be somewhat rare members of the community, especially in towns. I quickly realised why the CID trusted no one.

Shackleton explained that, when investigating a crime, we had to have a very, very open mind indeed and, difficult though it was to accept, we had to be suspicious of everyone, even the supposed victims. That sounds terrible on paper, but it is a fact of police life – some people do claim to be the victims of crime to cover their own crimes and deficiencies, and sometimes they do so in an attempt to gain revenge upon others. Police officers are taught to be very much aware of this tendency, especially when dealing with reports of rape or indecent assault by some women. We were mindful of Francis Bacon's works, 'Revenge is a kind of wild justice, which the more man's nature runs to, the more ought law to weed it out.'

In the police service, one soon learns that, in the world of criminal investigation especially, nothing must be taken for granted. The possibility of deviousness by members of the general public, particularly those with deep secrets of their own, must never be ignored or overlooked.

It was during this earnest and valuable talk with Shackleton that a call came through. Eltering Police Station's duty constable, PC John Rogers, came into the CID office from the enquiry counter. He was a calm individual; having done his job for years nothing surprised him or troubled him. In his quiet way, he had received calls about matters which would panic the most calm, terrify the fearless and horrify the sensitive. But John was unflappable, and he sailed through it all with characteristic equanimity.

'Ian,' he addressed Shackleton, 'we've a funny call just come in. A body's been found at Lover's Leap. It's a male. He's dead. He's been attacked, by all accounts. I've sent Echo Three Seven to the scene to investigate.'

'Genuine corpse, is it?' asked Shackleton.

'It could be a load of rubbish, of course, a false alarm probably with good intent. It'll be a tramp or a drunk sleeping in the sunshine; it's a tourist area.'

Rogers had received many reports of this kind, and I

recalled one of my own at Aidensfield. A motorist had reported a corpse lying on the side of a country lane, having apparently been knocked down by a hit-and-run car. When I went to investigate, I found a happy tramp fast asleep with his legs sticking out of the grass into the carriageway. I found it amazing that his legs had not been broken by passing vehicles, for he said he often lay down in this manner. It seems he loved to sleep on the grassy lanes of England. Such calls about corpses were all treated with a little caution, but all had to be dealt with.

'Where's Lover's Leap?' Ian asked.

'I can take you there. It's on my beat,' I said, recalling an incident involving a naked couple in a van who managed to set fire to the moor at that point.*

'Right, you'd better come with me, Nick,' said Shackleton, lifting his jacket from behind the door. 'John, if Gerry Connolly comes in, tell him where we are and what it's all about. Who found the supposed body, by the way?'

'A hiker. He rang in from a kiosk. He's waiting to show Echo Three Seven where it is. They're rendezvousing at the car park nearby – there's a picnic site there.'

And so we jumped into the CID car, a small red Ford Anglia, and headed for the splendour of the North York Moors. There were no blue lights to flash during this trip, no sirens to sound and no uniforms to indicate the importance of this journey. To all intents and purposes, we were just two men in a little car going about our routine business.

I showed Ian the route to Lover's Leap. It is a splendid beauty spot with stunning views across the surrounding

*See *Constable on the Prowl*.

moors and countryside. From a small plateau, the ground falls steeply away down a heather and bracken-covered hillside into a ravine. There are young pines and silver birches, and at the bottom of the ravine is a moorland stream of crystal clarity and icy coolness. The views embrace scores of scenic square miles. You can see the radomes of the Ballistic Missile Early Warning Station at Fylingdales, with the North Sea in the background, and in the valleys are tiny villages with church spires and cottages huddled beside streams or clinging to the steep-sided dales. It is a beautiful place and, as the name suggests, very popular with courting couples. They come at night, like moths flying towards a bright light, but this was a mid-afternoon in the early summer.

We arrived within forty minutes, and I could see the little police car, Echo Three Seven, waiting for us; two other cars occupied the parking area. The driver of Echo Three Seven, PC Steve Forman was standing beside it talking to a well-dressed man and to another in hiking gear. We halted, parked and walked towards them. Apart from this little party and the two cars, the picnic area was deserted.

Shackleton took control.

Forman told a simple tale. 'This is Stuart Finch,' he introduced the hiker. 'He was walking up the side of this hill, and when he was a few yards from the edge of the car park, he saw the man lying in the bracken. He spoke to him, got no reply, then touched him.' Finch nodded his agreement as Forman continued: 'He thought the man was dead, and so he rang us, and he had the sense to ring for a doctor.'

'Good thinking, Mr Finch,' said Shackleton. 'Well done.'

'And I'm Doctor Gregson from Malton,' the smart

man said. 'I've had a look at the man. He *is* dead. I'll confirm that, but I cannot certify the cause of death.'

'How long's he been dead, Doctor? Any idea?' asked Ian.

'Not long,' said Gregson. 'A couple of hours maybe. He's still fresh, no *rigor mortis*. I can't be more specific than that.'

'Any views on the cause then?'

'I didn't examine the body for marks – I thought I'd leave that to your experts – but it has all the appearances of a heart attack. The odd thing is that his clothes are in disarray, and that's a puzzle. Had his clothes been correctly worn, I'd have said it was nothing more than a heart attack, that he collapsed and died while walking here, although you appreciate I cannot certify that without knowing the casualty's medical history.'

There being no time like the present, Ian asked me to take a brief statement from the doctor before he left; he and the hiker, guided by PC Forman, went to examine the body.

I wrote the brief account of the doctor's findings in my pocket-book, and he signed it. I allowed Doctor Gregson to leave in his Rover and went to join the others at the corpse.

They were standing near the body when I arrived. I noticed a patch of smooth grass on a small, flat plateau in this sea of tall bracken; until one arrived at the patch of grass, it was impossible to see the body, so high and thick was the surrounding bracken. Finch had struck through the bracken to gain access to the car park and had found the dead man. It was almost pure luck that he had come by this route, for there was no formal footpath. Ian had quizzed him closely about his discovery and felt no suspicion could be attached to Finch.

I looked down upon the corpse. It was that of a heavily built man in his early fifties; he had an almost bald head with wisps of dark hair around the sides, a dark moustache and a soft, flabby face. He was lying on his back with his arms spread rather wide but his legs very slightly apart. He wore a light-coloured jacket and an open-necked shirt with most of the buttons undone, and his trousers were round his ankles, although it did seem an attempt had been made to draw them up. His white underpants were down too, and they stopped his legs from falling apart. I could understand Finch's thinking he had been attacked, but the odd thing was that a bunch of fresh sweet peas lay near his head.

Having quizzed the hiker and taken a written statement from him, Shackleton thanked him for his co-operation and allowed him to leave.

'So, what do we make of this?' asked Shackleton, puzzling as he stared at the recumbent form.

'Parked up there,' said Forman, 'there is a car that might be his, that blue Morris. A businessman, pausing for lunch maybe, was taken short and came down here because there's no toilets up there. Hence the dropped pants. Strained himself while at it, and his heart stopped?'

'That doesn't explain the sweet peas,' I said.

'They might not be his,' said Shackleton. 'Somebody else could have been here before him. Anyway, the point is: have we a natural-causes death or a suspicious one? If it's suspicious, we'd better notify the coroner and call in the cavalry – photographer, forensic pathologist, my boss, scenes of crime, the lot. We might have to set up a murder inquiry.'

'We'll need a PM to determine the cause of death,' I added for good measure.

'Right, decision time. We can't move the body until we have had it photographed *in situ*; I mean, it does look odd and I think we'd better treat it as suspicious. Right, Steve, radio Control, will you? Tell them we have a suspicious death here, and I'd like a senior detective to attend. Now, do we know who he is?'

'I haven't searched his clothing yet. I thought I'd better not touch anything. But that car might be his,' Steve reminded us of the blue Morris. 'You could do a check of the number for starters.'

'Nick, that's one for you.'

While Steve Forman made his call from Echo Three Seven, I went to examine the Morris. It was a blue saloon, two years old and in good condition; it was taxed and bore an excise licence issued at the North Riding Vehicle Taxation Office at Northallerton. This was before the days of the Police National Computer, but I knew we could discover the owner of the car very quickly through its registration number. I radioed Eltering from the CID car and gave them a situation report (a 'sit-rep'), then asked them to check the car number with the Taxation Department at Northallerton. It would take a few minutes, and in the meantime I took a closer look at the Morris, albeit without touching it. On the back seat were a briefcase and some coloured file jackets but I could see no names or identifying marks on them. Besides them was a length of floral wrapping-paper. I could see that it was printed with 'Gowers for Flowers' and a Scarborough address. And a solitary red sweet pea petal lay beside it.

Then I realised I knew this car. Or at least, I had seen it before. Because Lover's Leap was on my beat, I had made regular patrols to the locality over the past few months, and sometimes I had parked for a few minutes on the car park, both at night and during the daytime hours. And I was sure I had seen this blue Morris several times, always parked in this very place. I stood back from it now and walked away to the road, to gain the view I would normally see.

And the more I stared at it, the more I realised it was the same car, parked in precisely the same spot. But something was missing, some extra detail I had noticed before. And I could not recall that detail ... As I examined the scene before me, some parts of those memories came back to me, but not all, and I wondered if I had made a note of those occasions in my pocket-book. Recording such a sighting would hardly be necessary unless there was a reason, but I could not recall any official reasons for noting the registration numbers of cars parked here. Maybe this sighting had triggered off a memory of an incident in the past?

Then I heard my call-sign on the CID car radio: 'Echo Control to Echo One-Six.'

I lifted the handset of the CID car and responded: 'Echo One-Six receiving. Go ahead. Over.'

'Echo One-Six, reference your enquiry about the blue Morris, the registered owner is George Frederick Halliwell,' and I was given an address in Scarborough.

We could not assume that the dead man *was* Halliwell – this man might have borrowed his car – and we would now have to make enquiries in Scarborough to see if it could be him. We'd have to be very discreet, because we must not upset his relatives if Halliwell was still alive. A search of the body might confirm that name, but we would need a relative to come and view the corpse to make a formal, positive identification. That would be done when the body had been tidied up and placed in a mortuary.

Within an hour, the CID had arrived in a succession of vehicles. The force photographer, a detective chief inspector, scene-of-crime experts and other officers gathered to examine the body and commence their own specialist work.

The car park and bracken area were cordoned off as we awaited a forensic pathologist, and in the meantime official photographs were taken of the body, the location and the car, with its empty flower wrappings. The full might of a murder investigation was launched as the car park seemed suddenly full of police officers and official vehicles.

And then, as the formal investigation got under way, I remembered the circumstances of that blue Morris. About a year or eighteen months earlier, I had parked my police motor cycle here for a few moments during a patrol, and a woman had approached me with a purse she had found.

She'd found it on this car park a few moments before my arrival, and it had contained several pounds, a pair of silver earrings and other jewellery. As she was touring the area, she would not retain the purse, and so I entered it into our Found Property system. Before leaving the car park, however, I had approached the drivers and occupants of all the parked cars to see if it belonged to any of them. It did not – and the only two cars that remained empty were this blue Morris and a small green Austin mini.

I had noted the registration numbers of each, so that I could later trace the owners and contact them about the found purse. But before that need arose, a woman had reported losing the purse and it had been returned to her. I had never tried to trace the owners of the blue Morris and the green Mini. But I had noticed the green Mini parked beside the blue Morris on several successive occasions at the very spot, and those sightings had occurred over a period of around a year. The green Mini was not here today, it was not parked close to the Morris – and that was the missing item.

I would have to examine my old notebooks to trace those numbers but said nothing to the other officers at this stage, just in case my theories were incorrect.

The pathologist had examined the body and expressed an opinion that the fellow had been having sex with a woman immediately prior to his death. The flowers, the pants around the ankles and evidence of some seminal fluid found by the scientist supported that theory. The body, its mode of dress and position had all the hallmarks of such a situation.

In the pathologist's words, 'He was going at it hammer and tongs; he was right here with his fancy woman, just reaching the exciting bit, when his heart stopped. He literally died on the job, gents, and rolled off her, or she heaved him off, dead as a door nail. What a way to go. She's fled the scene, terrified … It's just a theory, mind, but I've seen it all before.'

'You mean this often happens?' smiled Forman, intrigued.

'Illicit affairs like this happen everywhere,' continued the pathologist. 'Poor old sod. You'd be surprised how many old codgers die on the job when they've found a young bit of stuff to keep their peckers up. But at least he died happy. I'll have to do a PM, but I'll bet my cotton socks it's natural causes, heart failure. The excitement was too much for him. If so, there'll be no need for an inquest, no need to drag his name through a coroner's court, or hers if you can find her.'

When the scientific examinations were finished, the

body was searched and a wallet containing a driving licence added strength to the belief that this was indeed the remains of Mr Halliwell, but we still needed a positive identification. And so the body was removed to a mortuary at Eltering as discreet efforts were made by Scarborough police to determine whether or not this was the late George Frederick Halliwell. A CID officer drove his car to Eltering Police Station, and the wrapping-paper was removed; Mrs Halliwell, if there was a Mrs Halliwell, would never see that scrap of evidence of her husband's unfaithfulness. The enquiries to confirm his identity had to be undertaken before his family was told of his death, and I wondered what the newspapers would make of it all.

I went home after a full day, and after my meal unearthed my old pocket-books. I searched every page for my notes on that purse and found them, having made the entry fifteen months earlier. The two car numbers were there – one agreed with that of today's blue Morris and the other was the green Mini. Tomorrow I would check that Mini number with the Taxation Department.

Next morning I learned that the man had been positively identified as George Frederick Halliwell. He was a county councillor and restaurant owner from Scarborough. His wife had had the awful task of viewing the body to confirm his identity, but she was not told of his reason for being at Lover's Leap. She was simply informed he had had a heart attack there, for that was the result of the pathologist's post-mortem examination. In other words, it appeared that his death was from natural causes, even if the circumstances were a little unusual. For us, the state of his clothing continued to be a worry, for it could be an indication of a struggle of some kind, instead of the aftermath of sex. Could his death be the result of manslaughter? Had there in fact been a struggle, a fight to the death? About a woman, even?

The morning paper carried a brief note of the death, saying only that we were investigating the death of a man found at a local beauty spot in Ryedale. The paper did not name Halliwell because, at the time of going to print, we could not confirm his identity. I was pleased that no sordid details were published. Having read the account, I rang Taxation and learned that the owner of the green Mini was a Mrs Dorothy Pendlebury, from a village near York, also a county councillor. I told Gerry Connolly of my findings.

'That's great, Nick, a real piece of detective work. Well done! Now, let's go and see her,' he said. 'You come with me, and we'll do it during the day, when her husband's at work. She'll never tell us if he's hanging around listening to every word. If she was the last person to see Halliwell alive, we need to know what happened.'

Dorothy Pendlebury was a tall, heavily built woman who was handsome rather than beautiful; in her early forties, she had a head of fine blonde hair and a bearing which could be described as almost aristocratic. In expensive clothes, she answered our knock and promptly assumed we were brush salesmen.

'I'm not seeing anyone today.' There was a haughtiness in her voice which was perhaps a means of covering her current uncertainty and misery. 'You'll have to see my husband if it's anything to do with the house, and he will be at work till seven.'

Gerry Connolly was all charm. 'Mrs Pendlebury, we are not salesmen, we are police officers,' and he introduced us by our names and ranks. 'I believe you knew the late George Frederick Halliwell of Scarborough, the restaurateur and county councillor.'

His opening words were designed to shock. There was but a moment's hesitation before she snapped, 'Yes, of course, I know him. We're on the county council, we serve on the same committees.'

'Mrs Pendlebury,' said Gerry in his quiet voice, 'I would like to have a word with you about him, in confidence.'

'Really? Why, might I ask?'

'I would prefer to talk inside the house if you don't mind,' continued Gerry.

She hesitated; I realised later that her mind must have been in turmoil at that moment, but her face never revealed anything of her emotions.

'I have an appointment in half-an-hour,' she said. 'I cannot break it ...' but she stepped back into the house and we followed her into the kitchen.

She indicated two chairs at the pine table but did not offer us coffee or tea.

'Well?' She stood near the window, looking out, her face away from our scrutiny. It was a clever move on her part.

I wondered how Gerry Connolly would tackle this interview, for I could guess she would deny any allegation he made. She was the sort of woman for whom appearances and social acceptance were of paramount importance, and any hint of a scandal, particularly a sordid sexual one, would be ruinous. There, in her mind, it would never happen – it had never happened ...

'I have reason to believe,' he said slowly, 'that you were the last person to see George Frederick Halliwell alive.'

Her head dropped slightly forward at this, but her face remained out of our sight as she gazed from her window.

'Is he dead?' her voice was hoarse now. 'No one told me.'

Gerry, in his soft, friendly voice, explained the circumstances surrounding the discovery of Halliwell's body, and he ended by repeating his earlier remark: 'I have reason to believe you were the last person to see him alive, Mrs Pendlebury. I have reason to believe you were with him at Lover's Leap.'

'We were good friends.' Her voice was a mere whisper now. 'He was a fine man ...'

'But yesterday were you with him at Lover's Leap?' Connolly stood up to ask the direct question.

'No!' she flung the answer at him. 'How dare you make such insinuations! I am a respectable married woman, the mother of two adult children, and a councillor; how dare you suggest that I was with him, on a secret liaison ...'

'I did not suggest any such thing, Mrs Pendlebury. I merely suggested you were the last person to be with him, to see him alive. You might have met there for business reasons, to discuss county council matters ...'

'I have nothing more to add, Inspector,' she snapped, and added, 'Now I must go. I have an urgent appointment to keep.'

Gerry stood his ground. 'Mrs Pendlebury, I need to know your movements yesterday around lunchtime. Mr Halliwell is dead, and his death is being investigated as suspicious. We know that he was not alone when he died.'

He allowed those words to register in her mind before he continued: 'And furthermore, we have every reason to believe that he was engaged in the act of sexual intercourse with a woman at the moment of his death. If that is true, his death will be regarded as being due to

30

natural causes – there will be no inquest and no publicity. If, however, we have to make more detailed enquiries, probably along the lines of a murder investigation, of course there will be publicity.'

He paused again to allow his words to take effect, then said, 'Now, so far as you are concerned, we could demand the clothes you were wearing yesterday, for fibres were found clinging to Mr Halliwell's clothes; we could ask you to submit to a medical examination to determine whether or not you engaged in sexual intercourse yesterday, and a forensic test might even confirm it was with Mr Halliwell … our forensic experts are very clever at matching stains and fibres – and we could make very searching enquiries about your movements over the past year or so.'

She did not say a word but remained on her feet, staring out of her kitchen window; she was totally composed and in command of her own emotions.

'If he did die in the manner you describe,' she said quietly, 'and if his death was due to a heart attack, there will be no inquest, no publicity? That is what you said?'

'That's true. But we do need to know the truth, and we will respect anything confidential.'

'I'll make some coffee,' she said suddenly, moving across to the cupboard for some mugs. Connolly winked at me but said nothing more as she busied herself in the kitchen. Finally, with three steaming mugs in her hands, she settled at the table, tearless and utterly composed, and faced Detective Sergeant Connolly.

'What do you want me to say, Inspector?' she asked.

'Just the truth,' he said.

'I panicked,' she licked her lips now. 'I ran away and I am ashamed of that; I am not ashamed of my liaison with him. I needed him and he needed me; there was no love, no risk of marriage breakdowns on either side, just sex. We fulfilled each other, Inspector, we made each other happy. Yes, I was with him yesterday, and yes, we were making love when he collapsed. I did my best to revive him but failed. Then I heard someone climbing towards us through the bracken, so I ran away, leaving him to find George. I recognise a heart attack when I see one. So what happens next?'

'I need a written statement from you, to complete my investigation – I need no more than what you have just told me.'

'But will it reach a court of any kind?'

'No,' he promised her. 'I must submit a report to the coroner, but as you have explained how he came about his heart attack, how you were present at his death, and as the pathologist's findings agree with your story, there will be no inquest. His death will be recorded as natural, not suspicious.'

'His wife will have to be told that he died during an act of adultery, will she?'

'No,' said Connolly. 'She has been told he died at Lover's Leap, but we have spared her the details.'

'And my husband?'

'He need never know of your involvement unless you tell him.'

'I will not tell him,' she said. She paused a long time as she sipped her coffee, then continued: 'You must both think I am evil, leaving him like that, running away, but I knew he was dead. I was a nurse, you know. I ran off to protect him from scandal. There was nothing I could do, nothing could be done to save him, and he did give me pleasure and happiness, and I gave it to him. There is nothing wrong in that, is there, Inspector? Not when you have an impotent husband ...'

'We are not concerned with the moral aspects of your relationship, Mrs Pendlebury, just the facts. Now, can we get this statement written down officially?'

'Yes, of course,' and I thought I detected a note of relief in her voice.

But there were no tears, no signs of sorrow and no hint of any regret. She was an amazing woman and I did wonder whether the hinted aristocratic breeding in her bearing was genuine. Whether she would cry when we left, I could not say, but she did not mention her appointment any more. Instead, she allowed Gerry to write down her statement, and it catered for those final minutes of George Frederick Halliwell. As he had rolled off her, dead but happy, she had tried to re-establish his clothing for decency's sake, but the weight of his body had defeated her.

She bade us farewell, still addressing Gerry as 'Inspector', and we were all relieved.

'I wonder why she left the sweet peas behind,' said Gerry as we drove away.

'They were probably her wreath,' I said. 'She won't attend the funeral, will she?'

'She will,' he said firmly, 'but as a county councillor and a colleague, not as his mistress. She will regard that as her duty,' he smiled.

'You know, Sarge, I think you are right,' I added.

And he was. She turned up at the funeral looking splendid and self-assured, but sorrowful. And she donated another wreath, this time without any sweet peas.

Chapter 3

The law's made to take care o' raskills.
                    GEORGE ELIOT (1819-80)

DURING ONE OF THOSE quiet moments in the CID office, it dawned on me why I might have been selected as an Aide to the constabulary's detectives. It was surely the outcome of two cases in which I had been involved during my very youthful days. At the time I was patrolling a town beat as a raw and unconfident constable at Strensford, but my actions had been recorded in my personal file and, indeed, I received a chief constable's commendation following one of the investigations. I guessed that, on the strength of these, I was thought to possess Sherlockian qualities, and so these cases are worthy of record here, even though they did not occur during my attachment to Eltering CID.

The first story began one New Year's Eve. In the North Riding of Yorkshire, this is a time of celebration. There are lots of parties, dancing, feasting, drinking and general *bonhomie*. As the desire to have a good time manifests itself in constables as well as ordinary mortals, most of us tried to avoid working night shift as the old year became the new one. Often lots were drawn to avoid argument and hints of favouritism but even then there were grumbles. To be off duty on New Year's Eve was indeed a bonus; to be on duty was a real chore.

On this particular New Year's Eve, a colleague of

mine, who was doing his best to woo the lady of his dreams, had an invitation to a dinner dance with her family. He desperately wanted to go. The sergeant said he could have the night off provided someone worked his night shift for him. He asked me. At first I was horrified at the thought but, with an understanding wife who was a close friend of his lady-love and who wished to see a successful conclusion to this ardent wooing, I capitulated. We swapped shifts and I found myself patrolling the deserted streets to the sound of happy people making merry behind closed doors. There is something akin to real distress within one's soul while patrolling a town alone, listening to the sounds of happy voices in warm interiors along every street. It produces a massive feeling of being unwanted, and it echoes the loneliness of the diligently patrolling police officer.

In spite of being on duty as the old year became the new, we did have a good time. In the chill of that happy night, girls kissed us to wish us a Happy New Year, we honoured the time-old tradition of First Footing* and we joined in many parties, albeit with the decorum of the constabulary uppermost in our minds. We regarded it as a good public relations exercise, a social mingling of the police and the people whom they serve and for whom they care.

By two o'clock that morning, with the first hours of the new year now history, it was snowing. The fall was gentle but it was dry, and it rapidly covered the ground with a blanket of beautiful white. Soon the entire landscape was glistening in the flickering lights of partying households and traffic-free streets, but we knew that on the lofty moorland roads there would be drifting in the bitter north-east wind.

*See *Constable Around the Village*

My refreshment break that cold morning was timed to begin at 2.15 a.m. and to finish at 3 a.m. I welcomed the warmth of the police station with its blazing coal fire, a blaze that was never allowed to go out between 1 October and 31 May. It burned for twenty-four hours a day, and it was a wonderful tonic during a chill night duty. I settled down with my bait-bag, which contained my snack of sandwiches and an apple, plus a flask of coffee. My only companion was the office duty constable, Joe Westonby. We chatted about the cheerful events of the night; even Joe had had visitors from the nearby houses, people who came in to wish him a Happy New Year in his lonely job.

And then, at 2.30 a.m., the telephone rang. It was the ambulance station, who announced they had received a telephone call from a moorland farmer to say that a car had overturned in his gateway and two people had been injured. They were now in the farmhouse but not too seriously hurt. He added that the moorland roads were treacherous and filling in rapidly with heavy drifting and a steady fall of snow, but the ambulance had to make an attempt to cover those five hilly moorland miles and bring the casualties to hospital.

'Take one of our lads with you,' Joe suggested to the ambulance station's duty officer. 'If it's not urgent, he can be with you in five minutes.'

This step agreed, partly to assist us in our duty of dealing with the accident and partly because in those days we did not have the regular use of official cars, Joe rang PC Timms at a kiosk in town and told him to accompany the ambulance. He suggested he take a shovel too, and some wellies, as it could develop into a hazardous trip.

With that drama now being dealt with, I resumed my

town patrol and returned to the office at 4.30 a.m. for a warm-up before the lovely fire. The sergeant said we could all come in for a break as we were covered in snow and our extremities were freezing. The steady pace of patrolling a beat does not warm the circulation, and it is not dignified to break into a trot, even on the coldest of Yorkshire nights. My toes and fingers were frozen, and I was ready for bed, but there was another hour and a half before I could book off duty at 6 a.m.

As I entered the station, I saw the ambulance struggling up the slippery slope to the hospital; it had to pass the police station to get there, so I grabbed a shovel and scattered gravel along its path. But it halted outside. 'There's snow up yonder that'll block us in before sunup,' said the driver. 'We nearly got snowed up in t'farmhouse. Anyroad, we made it; one of 'em'll need hospital treatment, t'other's in t'back with your mate. T'car's a write-off.'

I opened the rear doors of the ambulance and out climbed PC Graham Timms and another man. In the darkness, the ambulance struggled to finish its journey to the hospital with spinning wheels and a few sideways slithers as I accompanied Timms and his companion into the station. He had brought the man in so that he could obtain the details for his accident report.

Even in the gloom, I recognised the motorist and he recognised me; we had been brought up in neighbouring moorland villages, and in those small communities we all knew each other.

'Now then, Ben,' I said. 'You're not hurt then?'

'Hello, Nick. No, I was lucky. Harry's got a broken arm, I think. It could have been worse.'

'Who was driving?' I asked, merely out of interest.

'Me,' said Ben Baldwin as I followed him down the

dark passage into the enquiry office.

As he walked into the light of the office, I saw that he was wearing a smart pale blue raincoat that was a shade too long for his short figure and more than a shade too wide at the shoulders. As he and PC Timms settled into the office, with Timms arranging a cup of tea for Baldwin, I was sure I recognised that coat. It was exactly like one that had been stolen from a village dance hall about two years earlier. Baldwin took it off and hung it on a hook on the office wall, so I poured myself a cup of tea and studied it carefully. Baldwin was taken into another office by Timms, and I was alone with PC Westonby.

'Joe,' I said, 'that coat hanging there, I'm sure it's one that was stolen two years ago from a dance hall at Fieldholme.'

'Don't be daft, Nick,' he grinned. 'A coat's a coat. You can't tell one from another, especially not after two years!'

'I can,' I confirmed. 'Because it's mine.'

'Yours?' he puzzled. 'You mean somebody nicked your coat and this is it?'

'Yes,' I said.

He stared at me, unbelieving, then said, 'Try it on while Baldwin's out.'

I did, and it fitted perfectly; I knew it was mine. I returned it to the coat hook.

'Tell me more,' invited Joe.

I explained that, before I joined the police service, I did my two years National Service with the RAF and upon leaving bought myself a smart new raincoat. It was expensive, and it was RAF blue in colour. With my new coat on, I took my fiancée to a dance at Fieldholme Village Hall one Saturday night. It was during the three weeks holiday I had allowed myself between leaving the RAF and joining the police force. When the dance was over, I went to the cloakroom for my coat. It had gone. In its place there was a filthy brown raincoat that was covered in grease and oil stains and which was far too small for me. I reported the theft to the village constable.

'And you maintain this is yours?'

'Yes,' I said, without a shadow of doubt in my mind.

'But how can you tell?' he asked me.

'I dunno,' I had to admit. 'I just know it's mine – the colour's unusual for one thing, and it's too big for Baldwin anyway. That is my coat, Joe, and he's pinched it.'

'That's no good for our purposes, Nick,' he said. 'You know very well that we need to *prove* it's yours. Believing is no good; if we try to prosecute him on your say-so, no court would convict him.'

'So he gets away with theft of my coat?'

'Look, Nick, you know the ropes as well as I do. I know this seems different because you claim it's yours, but look at it on a broader plane – after all, anyone could claim property in this way, by merely saying it's theirs. People do make mistakes, you know. They think they recognise something they've lost ...'

I was aware of the problems and the need for positive identification, and in this case it highlighted the value of having some means of personalizing one's goods, especially when there are hundreds or thousands of identical copies.

'I've still got the brown one at home,' I said. 'I've been keeping it in case this sort of thing happened – I guessed the thief was local.'

'I'll have a go at Baldwin when Graham's finished with him,' promised Joe. 'You'd better not be the one to interview him – you're biased! In the meantime, I'll dig out your crime complaint – when was it, exactly?'

I told him the date of the dance two years earlier.

When Baldwin had given his account of the accident, Timms brought him back into the enquiry office to collect his raincoat. I stood to one side as Joe said, 'Put that coat on, Mr Baldwin.'

He did; it looked huge.

'Nice coat,' said Joe. 'Where did you get it?'

'Middlesbrough,' said Baldwin.

'New, was it?'

'Yes, brand new, but I can't remember the shop.'

'What did it cost?'

'Twenty-five quid,' he said; it had cost me £30, in fact.

Joe looked at me. How could we disprove this story? It lacked any detail that could be challenged – like the familiar thief's tale that 'I got it off a chap in a pub' or 'It fell off the back of a lorry.' I said nothing, knowing that I could jeopardise the enquiry if I wasn't careful.

Joe must have believed my claims because he tried shock tactics. 'Well, Mr Baldwin, I don't believe you. And I'll tell you what, you've just dropped the biggest bollock of your life. That coat isn't yours, it's this lad's. It belongs to PC Nicholas Rhea, and you nicked it from a dance hall at Fieldholme two years ago.'

Baldwin's eyes showed his guilt and his horror, but he recovered quickly and said, 'Bollocks! It's mine and I bought it new.'

Then I remembered a detail which no one else knew. It came to me as Baldwin was affirming his ownership, and I said, 'Joe, there is a way of proving it's mine.'

'You need something good, Nick,' was all he said.

'It is.' I was confident now. 'When I was in the RAF,

40

we had tags bearing our service numbers; we sewed them into our clothes. My number was 2736883, and it was on a white tag; I had some of those tags spare when I left the RAF, and I sewed one under the flap on the wrist of the right sleeve of that coat.'

I saw by the expression in Baldwin's eyes that he knew I was the true owner of that coat, but I also reckoned he would never admit stealing it. I had known him long enough to know his character, but had he found that tag?

Joe beamed. 'Come here, Mr Baldwin,' he said, and as Baldwin stood before him, Joe loosened the button on the flap on the cuff of the right sleeve and turned it back. But there was no service number tag inside – although there were some tiny remnants of white cotton where it had been removed.

'Evidence of guilt, Nick,' said Joe, pointing to the shreds of cotton. 'He's removed the number – that's good enough for a court.'

We looked at Ben Baldwin, guilt all over his face as he said, 'Sorry, Nick, I had no idea it was yours ...'

And he confessed to the theft two years earlier.

Due to my personal interest in the case, it was unwise for me to undertake the formalities that ensued. I was merely a witness, a victim of that crime, so Joe arrested Ben and he was formally charged. But it did not end there.

The first problem was that there was no record of my original report of the theft. The crime records did not show that I had reported it, and this threatened to cause administrative problems until the CID realised the entry might be in the lost-property book! And so it was. My coat was recorded as 'lost', not stolen, but at least there was a note of it in official records. But how on earth anyone could assume it was 'lost', when another of

41

completely different size, colour, appearance and quality had replaced it, was baffling.

I reckoned it was one way of keeping down the crime figures!

But there were more developments. When the local crime records were searched, it was learned that several other coats had been stolen from dance halls in the locality. They had disappeared over four or five years, and with the arrest of Ben Baldwin, we now had a prime suspect. He was a part-time barman and general dealer, who lived alone in a small cottage at a village called Kindledale. As common law permitted, the CID decided that his home should be searched for material evidence of those other crimes. Ben was told of these plans and did not object, so the search went ahead while he was in custody at Strensford.

If he had objected, a search warrant would have been obtained, although it was not necessary in these circumstances. The Royal Commission on Police Powers and Procedures expressed an opinion that the authority for such searches of the premises occupied by arrested persons was now enshrined in common law.

And in this case no further coats were found. But Ben's home did reveal a huge cache of other stolen goods. It was filled to overflowing with tins of food, bottles of whisky, brandy and gin, bottles of beer and stout, packets of sugar, flour and cereals and a host of other odds and ends. When confronted with this, Ben admitted stealing the lot from the various inns and hotels where he had worked.

In many instances, the owners had not missed the goods, although, with the volume involved, it was felt that any stocktaking would reveal these deficiencies. And so Ben was charged with several more thefts; as we say, these were 'TIC'd' when he appeared in the magistrates' court to answer the charge of stealing my coat. A hefty fine was imposed upon him.

The newspapers were full of the story due to the odd circumstances which had led to his arrest, and I had my coat returned to me, a little more battered and worn than it had been when I 'lost' it but still wearable after a thorough cleansing. And for my powers of observation in recognizing the stolen coat, I received a commendation from the chief constable.

But the story continues. A week after the court case, my wife's cousin rang me from Fieldholme. A large cardboard box had mysteriously appeared in his garden overnight, and when he opened it, it contained several overcoats. One belonged to him but he had no idea to whom the others belonged. Our records showed they had all been stolen in that vicinity.

And we never did find out who had stolen those other coats, nor who had dumped the box in that garden.

Some twenty years later, there was a further sequel to this yarn. I appeared before a Promotion Board at Police Headquarters where my career was discussed; that commendation was mentioned and I had to give an account of it. It was only as I discussed it with the chief constable and his senior officers that it dawned on me that nowhere in the Headquarters files was it mentioned that it was my own coat.

Maybe, if that early report had included that point, I would never have been commended?

However, it is clear that, if I had not swapped shifts that New Year's Eve, a lot of crimes would have remained unsolved.

The second investigation which came my way as a youthful constable at Strensford was one which involved 'discreet enquiries'. In this case, our neighbouring police force at Middlesbrough had received an application from a gentleman who wished to be granted a liquor licence. His request was for the grant of a restaurant licence which was issued by the justices.

He had bought some small parts of an old factory premises and wanted to turn them into a licensed restaurant. At that time, restaurant licences were a new idea, having recently been given statutory approval, for it meant that intoxicants could be sold with table meals away from the established hotels and inns, provided the premises were suitable and, of course, that the applicant was also suitable.

It was known that the applicant's expansive plans included future development of the site until it became a noted club, restaurant and even gaming centre. But all that was in the future – his immediate concern was to be granted that first liquor licence so that his restaurant could become a reality and so that he could establish himself on his chosen site.

He had submitted his plans and his application through the proper channels, and the role of the police, in forwarding these to the magistrates, was to establish whether or not he was a 'fit and proper' person to hold such a licence. He had no criminal record, and so it seemed his fitness to be granted such a licence was not in doubt. But, because he had given an address in Strensford, which was in a police area different from the one through which he was applying, we had to make discreet enquiries in the town. These were merely to strengthen his fitness claim; it was a routine enquiry for us, one of many we had to make.

At the start of my late shift one morning, Sergeant Andy Moorhouse called me into his office.

'Nick,' he said, holding a sheaf of papers, 'I've a grand job here for you. It involves some discreet enquiries and you can take a day or two over it; there's no rush, so long as you do a thorough job.'

He explained about the application for the restaurant licence and said, 'The applicant is a Mr Ralph Charles Swinden; he's forty-one years old and a native of Wakefield. But it seems he lived in Strensford for a year or two, and has given an address in town – No. 7 Belford Place. He doesn't live there now, by the way, but it seems he came to live there just over two years ago. We've been asked to make discreet enquiries in the area to see if there's any reason why he should not be granted his licence.'

I said I understood, but he continued:

'Now, have you done one of these enquiries?'

'No,' I admitted.

'There's no problem with them at all. They're an interesting way of occupying your time. Swinden has no criminal record, so it's just a case of asking local tradesmen whether he's honest and trustworthy. Get around the shops and businesses near where he lived and see if they know anything against him. Be discreet, Nick, and then submit your report through me. OK?'

'We've nothing in our files, have we?' I asked.

'No,' he said. 'I've never come across the chap, and I've been here six years. I've had a word with CID and he's never crossed their paths. He's obviously led a decent and quiet life, but we need to convince Middlesbrough Police and their magistrates of that.'

I looked forward to my task and was allocated a beat which included Belford Place. I started immediately I had read the papers and decided my enquiries would begin with people in the area whom I knew and trusted.

The papers did not say whether Swinden had worked in Strensford or whether he had merely lived there and worked elsewhere, but if he had been a part of the town's social or business scene, I would soon find out.

I tried to determine where a man in his late thirties, as he would then have been, would spend his money or his time and decided to start with those pubs he might have used.

I entered the Golden Lion when it was quiet and after some small talk with the landlord asked him, 'Jim, do you know Ralph Swinden? He used to live in Belford Place; he came to live in the town just over a couple of years ago.'

'What's he look like, Mr Rhea? What did he do?'

'No idea,' I confessed. 'I've just got a name.'

'Sorry,' he said. 'Ralph; I can't recall having a Ralph in here as a regular.'

There were seven pubs, two hotels and one registered club very close to Belford Place but no one associated with them knew Swinden.

He was not a member of the registered club either, but the steward did know most of the locals on the town's social round, those who frequented the golf club, the British Legion and the Strensford Working Men's Club, as well as those who had joined the Rotary Club, the Round Table, the Lions and other similar organizations. The name of Ralph Charles Swinden did not feature in his memory, but I visited the secretaries of those clubs and organizations he had suggested, just to be certain. They did not know him either.

My first tour of duty was concluded without anyone's knowing my subject, and I found that odd.

'How's it going, Nick?' asked Sergeant Moorhouse as I booked off duty.

'No one knows him, Sarge,' I said.

'Good, then no one knows anything against him,' he beamed.

'I've more people to see.' I wanted him to know I had not finished.

'No problem. Keep at it, but don't overdo it!'

The next day I continued my enquiries, for I was becoming intrigued by this nonentity. Surely a man cannot live in a small town like Strensford for two years or so and be totally unknown? I reckoned that he, or perhaps his wife, would certainly shop in town. Close to Belford Place there was a grocer's shop, the Co-Op, clothes shops, a sub-post office, vegetable and fruit shops, jewellers, an electrical supplier, stationer, newsagent and bookshop, butcher and many more. I decided to ask at them all, including those who might have called at the house, such as the postman and milkman, as well as insurance agents and travelling salesmen.

And in every case I received a negative reply. No one knew the man.

Sergeant Moorhouse said it all confirmed the notion that there was nothing known against him, nothing that would make him an unsuitable candidate for a restaurant licence. But I was not happy. Someone in town must know him.

All the following day I continued asking at shops and business premises. I knew a solicitor and asked him; I knew a bank manager and asked him; the postman shook his head, and the milkman said he had never come across Swinden. I asked the local Catholic priest, the vicar, the Methodist minister and the Salvation Army captain, none of whom knew him, and I even asked my colleagues. I found that in my off-duty time I was

47

asking people if they had come across Ralph Charles Swinden, but no one had. After three days of doing nothing else, I had not found a single person who knew him. Sergeant Moorhouse felt this was a perfect situation, for in his opinion it indicated that Swinden was not a man who got himself into debt or into trouble or into conflict with others. He seemed such a quiet chap, law-abiding, honest and with integrity.

When the sergeant said I should submit my report accordingly, I asked for at least another day on the enquiry, for I had to find someone who knew the man.

'Tomorrow then, Nick. I can't let this go on any longer, son; you're not letting it become an obsession, are you?'

'No, Sarge!' I cried. 'I just want to find somebody who knows him. Don't you think it's odd that no one has come across him?'

'Not really,' he said. 'Some folks live very quietly and go about their lives in total anonymity.'

I hardly felt that such a style of life suited a man whose ambition was to run a thriving restaurant and club; in my view, such a life-style was more suited to a hermit than a businessman. Businessmen were rarely so elusive and unknown. I knew I must ask at the houses which adjoined his address.

Belford Place was a curious little assemblage of cottages at the end of an alley; in Strensford, those alleys are called either ghauts, ginnels or yards. They form a narrow tunnel through the houses or shops. Often with a roof at first-floor level, they reach from the streets and occasionally open into a small square around which the occupants dwell. The alleys leading from the streets are little wider than a pram, and indeed some have doors on the street so that the casual passer-by has no idea that a small community exists behind. In those instances where the alley does not open into a square, the cottage doors and windows line each side, so that people living opposite one another are almost within arm's length. But Belford Place did open into a small, irregular square; it was a pretty area with a handful of tiny stone cottages. They boasted bow windows and were built of local stone as they nestled in this quiet area just behind a busy thoroughfare. Apart from the alleyway between the houses, this place was virtually shut off from the world.

I counted eight cottages, all neatly painted, with polished numerals on the doors and colourful boxes of flowers adorning their window-ledges. The area between the cottages comprised paving-stones, and here and there were dotted half-barrels of more flowers. It was a very pretty little area, a picture-book kind of haven.

Being a methodical sort of chap, I started my enquiries at No. 1. Upon my knock, the door was opened by an elderly, stooping man whose eyes showed the initial horror that most people feel upon being unexpectedly confronted at their front door by a uniformed policeman.

I adopted an oblique approach to my search for information, for I did not want undue alarm or gossip to be created by my visit.

'I'm looking for a Mr Swinden,' I said. 'Ralph Swinden. I'm told he lives here.'

'Swinden?' shouted the old man. 'Never 'eard of 'im. Where's 'e live then?'

'In one of these houses,' I responded.

'You've got it wrong, lad,' he grunted and went back inside.

And so I tried No. 2, where a middle-aged lady, holding a ginger cat in her arms, told me she had noticed a man at No. 7 who disappeared for long periods but she didn't know his name. At No. 3 I got a similar response from a young woman with a baby who'd recently moved in, while at No. 4 a huge woman eating a bread bun produced a negative result. The man at No. 5, who looked like a holidaymaker with his colourful shirt and open-toed sandals, said he was just visiting the yard and had never heard of Swinden. The lady at No. 6 refused to open the door, but shouted her answers through the letter-box. I think I'd got her out of the bath. I omitted No. 7, which was Swinden's supposed address, but got the now expected answer from No. 8; the couple living there, tiny folk with a tiny dog that yapped at my knock, shook their heads and said they had never known a Mr Swinden, but could it be that man at No. 7?

I was now left with No. 7. Should I ask there? I knew that these enquiries were supposed to be discreet, but I was now in a position where I had to know something, anything, about the mysterious subject of my investigation.

I decided to enquire at No. 7.

I rapped on the door and waited. My knock was answered by a woman about thirty-five years old. She wore a cheap frock with a flowery design and carpet slippers, and her fair, untidy hair was wet, probably having just been washed.

'Oh, the law!' she gasped when she saw me. 'What have I done?'

I smiled. Her approach was friendly enough, and so I went into my new routine. 'I'm looking for a man called Swinden, Ralph Charles Swinden ...'

Before I could go any further, she exploded. 'That bastard!' she cried. 'Where is he? What's he done now?'

'You know him?'

'You bet I know him! What's all this about, Constable?'

'Can I come in?' I asked, for I did not want this development to be overheard by the entire yard. She led me into a tiny kitchen, where she had obviously been washing her hair over the sink, for shampoos and towels lay on the draining-board. 'Sorry about the mess, I've just been tarting myself up. Coffee?'

'I'd love one.' I was ready for a sit-down after my perambulations, and this promised to be a revealing discussion. She made us each a mug of instant coffee, sighed heavily and then settled opposite me at the formica-covered kitchen table.

'So,' she said, shovelling three spoonfuls of sugar into her mug, 'what's he been up to?'

'Before I tell you, how do you know him?' I wanted to establish the truth of this little affair right at the start.

'He was my lodger,' she said, and I guessed the term was merely a euphemism.

'So you are not Mrs Swinden?' I asked.

'Not likely!' she said. 'I wouldn't have him for keeps.'

'So who are you?' I had to ask.

'Smithson, Jenny Smithson,' she smiled. 'And this is my house, not his. My dad left it to me; it's all mine.'

'Do you work?' I asked.

'Part-time. I'm a barmaid at the Mermaid Hotel most evenings, and then some days in the week I serve behind the counter at Turner's – that's the fruit and veg shop near the harbour.'

As I paused to write down these details in my pocket-book, she asked, 'So what's all this about?'

I was a little uncertain how much I should explain, but if this woman's description of 'lodger' was true, I

51

could ask my 'discreet enquiries' of her. If lodger meant live-in lover or common law husband, it might be different. I decided to be honest with her; after all, she was the only person in the town who admitted knowledge of Swinden.

'He's applied for a liquor licence in Middlesbrough,' I began. 'He wants to open a restaurant, and he has given this as his former address. My job is to enquire around here to see if he is a fit and proper person to hold such a licence.'

'He most definitely is not!' she burst out. 'Oh, my word, no! Look, Constable, let me show you something.'

She went into her living-room and I heard her open a cabinet of some kind, then she returned with a small book.

'Right,' she said. 'This is my building society passbook. See that last entry?'

She handed it to me and I saw there had been a withdrawal of the entire funds, totalling £203.17s.6d.

'So?' I asked.

'He did that, Constable. He forged my signature on the withdrawal form and got away with all my savings. And he pinched money from upstairs – I keep my spare cash in a vase in my bedroom, and that's all gone. Fifty quid or so.'

'How did this happen?' I put to her, sipping the coffee.

She explained how Swinden had met her during her work in the Mermaid, and they had struck up a liaison. He had been seeking accommodation in Strensford and so, eventually, she had taken him into her home, at first as a lodger, but it wasn't long before he was in her bed too. This had happened about two years ago, and they had been moderately happy. He said he was a salesman, and so he was away quite a lot. Then she had to go to Reading to look after the two children of her sister who was ill; she had spent some six weeks there earlier this year, leaving Swinden in the cottage to care for himself. And when she had returned, only last week, he had gone; there was no note to explain his absence, but all his things had been removed and he had left no forwarding address.

'I came back unexpectedly,' she said. 'I thought I'd be away for six months or even more, and so did he. Maybe that's why he gave this address, thinking no one would be here? Anyway, here I am, back at home.'

'So what did you discover?' I asked.

'Only yesterday,' she continued, 'I went to find that passbook; I was going to buy myself a new dress and I found my money had all gone. When I asked at the building society, they said they had a withdrawal form, signed by me, and they refused to think someone else had done it. Well, somebody else has, Constable, because I was in Reading at the time of the withdrawal. Is that something you can investigate? I was wondering if I should call in the police about it.'

'Yes,' I said. 'We can investigate, and it *is* something you should make an official complaint about.'

Sergeant Moorhouse was surprised, to say the least, the CID were delighted to have a forgery to investigate and the superintendent was somewhat aghast that my discreet enquiries had uncovered this crime.

Ralph Charles Swinden was not granted his restaurant licence, the reason being that his conviction for forgery and larceny, with its heavy fine and the order for restitution of the missing cash, meant he was not a fit and proper person.

Chapter 4

You thought you were here to be the most senseless and
fit man for the constable of the watch.
Don Pedro: *Much Ado About Nothing*
WILLIAM SHAKESPEARE (1564-1616)

'ON OBBO' OR 'KEEPING obs', is the police jargon for
'keeping observations'; this means watching a suspect
person or premises, and it usually entails long, cold and
boring hours alone and in silence while accommodated
in the most cramped of conditions. We could be hunched
in the back of a bare and cold van or car, we could be in
a filthy, draughty loft watching the street below or we
might be hidden in a wood or field with only the owls,
foxes, weasels and voles for companionship.

Many of these long stints ended with no positive
result, but sometimes the rewards can be great, such as
those occasions when one catches a suspect bank-raider
or burglar. For that reason, there is always the
excitement of the unknown, and this helps to sustain the
observer during those worst soul-destroying times.
During a long obs session, there is something of the
gambler's tension, for one literally never knows whether
the anticipated result will occur. Some you win, some
you lose. If you win, you are exhilarated; if you lose,
you know there'll be another obs job along in a moment
or two, one that could produce better results and the

exhilaration of catching a villain in the act of committing his crime.

'We've an obs job for you,' said Gerry Connolly to me one morning. 'Tomorrow night, mebbe all night. Come on duty at ten o'clock, dress in something dark and warm, and fetch a flask of coffee and some sandwiches. Oh, and a torch. I'll fill you in tomorrow. There'll be a briefing at ten o'clock.'

Apart from demolishing my assurance to Mary that I would not be expected to undertake night duty when working as a CID Aide, this also caused some *angst* in her because she had no idea what I was about to do. Neither had I, so I could not explain, but policemen's wives do learn to be trusting and understanding. They have to be when neither knows what is about to happen or what involvement there will be. In some cases there can be danger, and well they know it.

'I've no idea what I'll be doing or how late I'll be,' I said as I dressed in some old black uniform trousers, several dark sweaters and a pair of black leather gloves. 'They didn't say what the job was; nobody knows. We're to be briefed when we report for duty.'

'Just be careful then.' She kissed me goodbye. 'It does sound dangerous, all those dark clothes ...'

'They're the warmest I've got,' I said, trying to be nonchalant. 'Bye.'

I arrived at Eltering Police Station to find five other detectives, all dressed in thick, warm clothes. I knew two of them, for they had been drafted in from Strensford, but the others were strangers to me.

As we assembled in the main office, wondering what our mission was to be, Detective Sergeant Connolly came in.

'Right,' he said. 'Into the court house, all of you;

we'll have our briefing there.'

The court room adjoined the police station, and there was a linking passage; no one would be using it at this time of night, and so it offered some security from flapping ears. Ears can flap in police stations, ears that can unwittingly – or sometimes deliberately – reveal the secrets of an undercover operation. This was clearly an operation of paramount secrecy, so secret that even other police officers were not to be informed. We were therefore the elite of the moment, those in the know, those selected for a mission of sensitivity and drama, an occasion to display our professional skill and competence. We all wondered what on earth was going on. When we were seated, Gerry Connolly gave each of us a thin file containing a diagram of a street, a plan of some houses in that street, and a list of other details such as the names, car numbers and distinctive marks or habits of those whom we were soon to learn were suspects.

'Has everyone got a file?' he asked, and when there were no dissenters, he continued: 'Right. This is our task for tonight. It will be known as Operation Phrynia.'

'Frinia?' puzzled one of the men.

'Phrynia,' affirmed Gerry Connolly without explanation. He paused as he took the street plan from his own file. 'Examine the street plan first ...'

As he spoke, we learned that the street was Pottery Terrace, Eltering. It lay in the older part of the town where, as the name suggested, there had once been a thriving pottery. The house in which we were interested was No. 15. It was a terrace house built of local stone with a front door leading directly onto the street, and a back door opening onto a closed yard. The exit from the yard led into a back lane.

'No. 15 Pottery Terrace is the home of Margot Stainton, Mrs Margot Stainton, who is thirty-two years old. Her husband is a squaddie serving in Germany, a tank regiment, I'm told, and when he's away, she gets lonely and so she goes on the game. We don't think he knows what she gets up to. She is helped in her enterprise by some of her lady friends, who, we are assured, are very enthusiastic volunteers who earn a bob or two for their efforts. That house, gentlemen, is a knocking shop, and it is attracting customers from a wide area, some of whom will make headlines if we catch them at it. It is a brothel, gentlemen, not a high-class one by any means, but a busy one if our information is correct.'

He paused to let us digest these words and went on:

'The house is jointly owned by Mr and Mrs Stainton, which means she can be prosecuted for keeping or managing the brothel; there is no question of a landlord or agent being involved. So it is our job tonight to prove that she is running a brothel.'

Most of us were now striving to remember the law on brothels, but Gerry was continuing.

'Our purpose tonight is to gain the evidence which will, in the long term, justify a prosecution and secure a conviction. We also need to acquire sufficient evidence to enable us to obtain a warrant to search the premises and to arrest any suspects. That will be the second phase of this operation; tonight we are to be engaged on the first phase, the observations which will give us the evidence we need to justify the second phase. We are prepared to keep obs for two, three or more nights if necessary. We have had complaints from neighbours, by the way, and so we want to clean up this terrace.'

He then reminded us about the law on brothels: we

had to prove that at least two women were using the house, or just a room in the house, for the purposes of illicit sexual intercourse or acts of lewdness. If just one woman was using the house for those purposes, however much she charged or whatever number of men she coped with, that was not a brothel. Two women were required in law if we were to prove the house was a brothel, but it did not matter whether or not they were paid for their work.

We had to make a note of the number of men arriving at the premises, with times and modes of transport (and car registration numbers where possible), the number of women in the house at any one time and, if possible, evidence of what they got up to when they went into the house.

A raid of the house was not planned tonight, he told us; that might come later, once the evidence had been obtained to justify it. He paused again for all this to sink into our skulls, for it was now time to allocate individual tasks. We were all given particular places to hide in, so that all entrances and exits were covered, and there was to be no radio contact with Eltering Police Station or the force control room. Our duty was simply to note everything and everyone we saw entering and leaving that house, with names if possible, conversations and other factors that would establish its role as a brothel. We were to remain at our allocated points from 11 p.m. until 2 a.m. At 2 a.m. we were to stand down, without orders being given, and we had all to rendezvous in the playground of the infants' school just around the corner. If for any reason the operation was aborted earlier, we were to rendezvous in that playground. There would be a brief résumé of our success or otherwise, and we would then return to Eltering Police Station to write up our notes.

As the positions were allocated, I awaited mine with interest. Finally, he said, 'D/PC Rhea. We've a special one for you. Now look at the plan of the house. Got it?'

'Yes, Sarge,' I said.

'You see the building that extends from No. 15 to abut the lane at the back? It makes the house L-shaped.'

'Got it,' I said.

'That is a one-storey-high set of outhouses. There's a washhouse, an outside loo and a coalhouse. All the houses in that terrace have them.' I knew the kind of building to which he referred; they were a feature of the terrace houses in this region. 'That building forms the boundary to the east; each of its doors opens into the yard of No. 15. The other side of that same building has another loo, coalhouse and washhouse, and they open into the yard of No. 13.'

'I get the picture,' I said.

'It would be nice if we could hide in one of those sheds to watch visitors, but we daren't; for one thing it would amount to a trespass by us, and for another they might use any of them tonight and discover us. So, Nick, I want you on the roof of that building. That way you will not be seen. There are no street lights in that back lane, and from that roof, if you lie on it, you will be able to look down into the yard of No. 15. All those houses have flat cement roofs, by the way, so there is no danger of falling through it or falling off it. From there, you'll be able to see all movements through that back entrance, and you should be able to overhear any conversations at the back door as visitors arrive and depart. Note everything in your pocket-book: times, names etc.

'Now, above you, if you stand with your back to the wall of No. 15, is the window of a back bedroom. We know that room is used by the incoming fellers and at least one of the women.' He paused and continued: 'It would be of enormous help to this operation if you could overhear any snatches of action or conversation in that room.'

'Won't I be seen up there?'

'Not if you're careful. I note you've dark clothing on, and you can climb onto the roof by shinning up the rear wall of No. 15's yard, from the back lane. It's a high roof, and if you keep still, you'll not be spotted. If you are seen, just run for it – jump into that back lane and gallop like hell. They'll think you're a pimper or a burglar. That applies to you all – this is an undercover operation, lads, so you're on your own. Think on your feet and keep out of trouble. Right? Now, any questions?'

There were one or two points of clarification and then we were despatched to our posts, one at a time to avoid what might appear to be a bunch of hooligans marching into town. I was the last to leave.

'Sarge,' I said to Connolly, 'one point of curiosity. Why call this job Operation Phrynia?'

'A joke of sorts, Nick; we shan't be using radios, so the lads needn't remember it. But Phrynia, or Phryne as she is sometimes called, was a famous Greek prostitute some 400 years before Christ. She was gifted with extraordinary beauty and, in fact, was the model for the statue of Venus rising from the sea. She was eventually tried for being a prostitute.

'She was defended by Hyperides; the evidence was all against her, and just before a guilty verdict was about to be given, he tore her robe to expose her magnificent chest. And at that, the judges' minds went berserk and they acquitted her. So beware the wiles of women and their lawyers, and beware of Mrs Stainton. Don't forget, she might claim you and the other lads are her customers...'

I made a resolution to remain very carefully concealed during my forthcoming duty and left the station. It was a cool, dark night with no moon and, in those areas away from the street lights, the town was pitch dark. I arrived at the rear of No. 15 on foot, knowing that I was being observed by hidden CID men. I looked for them but could not see them, so I reckoned no casual visitor would know of our observations.

At the rear door of No. 15, the one which led into the yard, I had the task of climbing onto the wall, which was about eight feet high, and then making my way onto the roof of the outbuildings. I dare not use my torch, which was stuffed into my pocket, but I found I could mount the wall by using the handle of the yard door in conjunction with some footholds in the stonework. It was a scramble, but in a short time I was lying stomach down on the wall – facing the wrong way. I then had to stand up on the narrow top of the wall in order to turn around and walk towards the roof upon which I was to spend the next three hours. It was like walking a tightrope but I reached the edge of the roof without falling off.

The wall upon which I had walked formed the end outer wall of the outbuildings. The edge of the roof was level with the top of the wall, and it would be a simple matter to transfer from one to another. But then I was horrified to find it was *not* a flat roof. These outbuildings had a sloping, tiled roof – all the other houses had flat-roofed outbuildings. Someone had not done their research very thoroughly! So I now had an additional problem.

I could see the slates ahead of me, shining in the meagre light from the houses, and that at this end, the back street end, the roof ended with stone copings which rose steeply from the wall. I was sure Connolly had said it would be a flat roof ... but orders were orders. In the gloom, I could see the ridge of the roof and saw that it extended to the back wall of the house. If I could creep along that ridge, I could sit there, straddling it with my legs as I kept observations. I had to prove I could do this job. Ahead of me, and joining the wall upon which I stood, was a steep slope of coping-stones which led up to the ridge. I must not step directly onto the tiles, and I knew I must climb up that slope.

Cat-like, I now began to climb towards the summit of the roof without standing on any of the blue slates. My gloved hands gripped the coping-stones at their edges as I inched my way upwards. And then I was at the top. If I crept onto the ridge now, I would be facing the wrong way, and so I decided to turn around.

I wanted to sit on the ridge of the roof with a leg dangling down each side, and my back could then rest against the wall of the house, beneath that bedroom window that was of such interest. With infinite care, and happy that no one was walking along that back lane to witness my efforts, I twisted and inched myself onto the roof. In my heavy clothes, I was perspiring by the end of my manoeuvring, but eventually I was sitting astride the ridge tiles which ran along the rounded peak of this well-built outhouse roof.

It was now time to inch my way backwards towards the house. I glanced at the bedroom window which was one of my objectives but it was not illuminated and it seemed the curtains were closed. I was not too late for that task – not yet, anyway.

By executing a kind of low-level rearward leapfrogging movement, I did journey backwards two or three inches at a time towards the security of the wall of the house. I was half way through my trip when someone approached; a man suddenly materialised in the rear alley. He opened the yard door, flitted into the yard and then walked purposefully towards the back door of the house. He knocked and waited as I sat on the roof watching him. I wondered how I could reach my pocket-book in the darkness to record this moment, but the door opened and a woman's voice said, 'Come in, Ken.' He vanished inside without seeing my right foot dangling upon the sloping tiles only a few feet above his head. I would make my notes when I was settled, but what I had observed was hardly criminal material.

Then another man came the same way; he was admitted by a woman who said, 'Come in, Alec. Nice to see you,' but I could not see her. I had no idea whether it was the same woman. I wondered if the front door was now busy receiving guests. (I was later to learn that some eight or nine men and a similar number of young women were in the house by this time, having used the front door.) When a third man arrived by this route, I began to wonder if I would ever reach the security of the wall behind me, for I was still marooned midway along. I remembered he was called Gordon.

I noted their times of arrival on my watch … 11.15 p.m., 11.19 p.m. and 11.22 p.m. Not knowing how many women were inside, nor how many men had entered through the front door, it seemed that an orgy was planned. But not for me. I was still inching backwards, trying to be silent, trying not to send tiles spinning into the yards at each side of me, and trying to be invisible.

Then my back touched the wall. I had arrived at my

place of safety. I felt very relieved at this achievement and was pleased that I could now sit here and observe. I leaned back against the welcoming wall, panting with my efforts and now feeling much more secure. For a few minutes nothing happened. I sat on my odd perch and gazed around the street scene below, my eyes now accustomed to the darkness and my ears attuned to the noises of the town.

I could hear faint music from somewhere too, a regular beat. And sometimes the sound of happy voices reached me, to provoke in me a sense of loneliness and isolation. What on earth was I doing, sitting on a roof as midnight approached, I asked myself. The ridge tiles, although rounded and made of clay, were most uncomfortable; after a few moments of sitting, I had to stretch my legs and relieve the discomfort, and I wondered if I could stand up, just for a few moments, to get my circulation moving and to ease my cramped muscles.

I decided to test the strength of the tiles. Gingerly, I placed each foot squarely upon a couple of tiles and allowed them to take my weight; they seemed to be firm enough. But to stand up, with my back against the wall, I needed some kind of assistance and recalled the window above me and to my right. There was a similar window to my left as well; it belonged to the house next door. If I could reach the window ledges, I could use them to lever myself to my feet, and they would offer some support. I extended my right arm high to my right, and in the gloom my finger reached the ledge. But this was not enough to give me the purchase I required; I therefore extended my left hand and found the other window-ledge. Now, with both hands, I tried again, but my right hand slipped an inch or two – there was moss on that window ledge. It was enough to throw me off balance for a fraction of a second, and in so doing my left hand slid along the neighbouring window-ledge.

And then drama.

That sliding hand hit a plant pot which stood on the ledge. I turned to look; in horror, I saw it topple off. But there was worse to come. That pot had been tied to another, and another ... there were six plant pots, all full of plants, and as the first one toppled off the ledge, its weight moved the others. And I was too far away to save them. One by one, they leapt off that ledge and crashed into the back yard of No. 13, strung together like rock-climbers, each falling away.

The first crashed into a coal bunker but the second, having escaped from its securing string, hit the window sill at ground-floor level; the third, I think, hit the metal dustbin with a resounding clang, and the others all crashed into various objects in the yard. The noise was terrible. I heard angry shouts from No. 13, and the back door opened. A large number of men poured out ...

One of them saw me.

How I achieved my next act, I do not know, but I galloped along the ridge of that roof as if I were a fleeing cat and leapt off it into the back lane seconds before the men burst from their own back yard. But to my surprise, they did not chase me – instead, they hurtled into the yard of No. 15. I heard shouts and curses, women screaming and the sound of men fighting ...

Within seconds, I saw the familiar sign of a blue light racing through the darkness and decided I should remain invisible.

I decided to head for the rendezvous point in the school playground, even though it was only just midnight. Within minutes of my arrival, the others turned up. The exercise had been aborted.

'What happened?' asked Connolly in the darkness. He did not address his question to me in particular but to anyone who might answer.

'Dunno,' said one of our men. 'There was a hell of a crash, and the next thing I knew, those five brothers from No. 13, and their dad, all burst into No. 15 and began knocking hell out of the men in there.'

'And what was happening at No. 15?' asked Connolly.

'A party, I think,' said one of the detectives. 'A birthday party, nothing more than that. No orgy, nowt. Just a party with lots of blokes and girls there, some good music and a fair bit of drink and noise. No brothel tonight, Sarge.'

Later, back at the station when the beat car returned after attending the rumpus, we were to learn that there had been bad feeling between No. 13 and No. 15 for years, and each had performed nasty tricks upon the other over a long period. The crashing plant pots had been thought just another in this war of aggravation because the people at No. 13, a family called Parry, had complained about the noise of the music only minutes before. They'd rung Margot Stainton and had issued a string of abuse down her telephone, so the police took no action.

In our terms, all the participants were warned as to their future conduct. The beat man had no idea that we had been keeping watch on the premises, but no further observations were kept upon that house and there were no more complaints about it.

But I never told anyone about my part in provoking that incident.

It is a feature of observations of this kind that one

branch of the service operates without the knowledge of the others, and there are many practical reasons for this, secrecy being, at times, of paramount importance. This practice was to cause problems at another obs job.

Detective Sergeant Connolly had received a tip from one of his many informants that a switch of high-value stolen goods was to occur at a place called Springbeck Farm. This was on the moors above Eltering, on the edge of a moorland village called Liskenby. According to his informant, there was to be a raid on a country house in south Durham on Friday evening when the occupants were out at a hunt ball. The raiders were intent on getting their hands on the family silver; they had an outlet for it, through some less-than-honest members of the antique trade in the Midlands and south, and so a system of transporting it to their crooked dealers had been arranged. The switch would be late on that same Friday night or in the early hours of Saturday morning.

Our information was that the unoccupied Springbeck Farm had been selected due to its remoteness. I often wondered how the CID managed to acquire such detailed information from informants, and I also pondered upon the motives of such informants. Without them, the work of the CID would be difficult, and yet the detectives who relied upon them despised them as much as the criminal fraternity hated them.

However, this information was regarded as 'good', which meant it had to be acted upon. And that meant a period of observation on the farm and its ranging buildings, with the utmost secrecy being observed. There could be some danger in this exercise, for men in possession of high-value goods are loath to relinquish them without a fight, but there was no question of being issued with firearms. We would have to make do with own strength and skill, aided by our detective staves, short truncheons which would fit into a jacket pocket.

Connolly decided that a visit to the farm for a recce was out of the question; the villains themselves might be keeping a watch on the premises, although a drive past the entrance in a plain car was agreed. Four of us undertook that mission. We discovered that a rough, unmade track led down to the farm from the moor road between Eltering and Strensford. Although the gate, bearing the name Springbeck Farm, was on the main road, the farmhouse and its buildings were out of sight in a shallow valley.

There was no road direct to the farm from the village of Liskenby, in whose parish the farm stood, but there was a second route into the buildings. That led from Liskenby Manor, the big house which was the focal point of Liskenby Estate. A private road led from the village through the estate and up to the big house, and a lane ran from that road to Springbeck Farm, which belonged to the estate.

'Whoever selected this spot knows that estate,' said Connolly. 'Not many farms have two entrances; in this case, they drive in off the main road, do the switch and drive out through that estate. And because the estate is private property, no member of the public is going to see vehicles moving around at night, and the big house is too far away from anyone there to notice them. So, let's make our plans. We'll all have to be involved in this one.'

There were several imponderables. We had no idea how many men would be involved; we did not know how many vehicles would be used, nor indeed what kind they would be. They might be stolen or hired for the job. They could be cars, vans, cattle trucks or pantechnicons, and we did not know precisely what time they would arrive. Our information did not tell us they would be armed, and so we had to assume they would not; in those days, not many villains did carry firearms. This meant a long period in hiding around the farm, but in this instance there would be radio contact, albeit using codes because some villains listened in to police broadcasts.

There needed to be a lot of careful planning. The dog section would be placed on alert too, without telling them why, and so would the traffic department. And they would be told to keep away from Liskenby and district unless ordered directly to take action there.

Our task was to catch the thieves or handlers in possession of the stolen goods; that was always first-rate proof of their villainy, for seasoned criminals were cunning enough to get rid of 'hot' goods as soon as possible or to deny they had ever been in possession of them. In this case, we felt that the transfer of goods would take place in a barn; the barns on these moorland farms were large enough to accommodate two furniture vans or certainly a couple of smaller vehicles. Even Dutch barns, especially when replete with hay or straw, offered some security. But no one knew the layout of these premises. We daren't ask either the estate or the local council's planning office for plans, due to the secrecy involved, and so we had to rely on our ability to think fast at the time.

After a lot of deliberation, which involved studying all the possible methods of tackling this problem, it was decided that the four of us, Connolly, Wharton, Shackleton and myself, would enter the farm buildings via the village; there was a footpath across the fields. Under cover of darkness, we could achieve that without being seen, and we would take portable radios. We would leave the car on the pub car-park; it was unmarked and would not attract attention there.

At the farm, we found a large and beautiful dwelling-house in a splendid setting, remote and, in the day time, with staggering views across the valley. All the doors were locked and the windows were secure; it was in very good condition in spite of its lack of use. In the adjoining yard, which had a concrete base, was a row of looseboxes and sundry small buildings. This had clearly been a stable block, and all the stable doors were closed and in good condition. There was a large barn but the doors were closed and secured with a huge padlock, while the Dutch barn did contain some bales of straw. In the darkness, we silently inspected the layout and ascertained, beyond all doubt, that the farm was totally deserted.

'Right,' said Gerry Connolly, 'I reckon they'll do the switch in that stable yard; the ground before the Dutch barn is too soft for a large vehicle to linger on it for long, and I doubt if they'll break into the barn. There are no other open buildings. And that stable yard has two ways in, or one way in and another way out. The surface is good, the buildings around it will offer some security and there's always the looseboxes to dive into if necessary.'

We listened to him and agreed with his comments.

'I think we ought to be in the Dutch barn,' he said. 'It'll provide us with cover, and we can see into the yard area of the stable block; we can also see the lights of any vehicles approaching. And we can move about fairly quietly.'

Once more, we all agreed. We adjourned to the Dutch barn and settled on the bales of straw, whereupon Connolly produced a flask of coffee and some chocolate biscuits. It was only ten o'clock in the evening, a chill autumn night, and there was a long time to wait.

Hardly had we sipped our taste of coffee when things started to happen. Lights appeared across the fields; a vehicle of some kind was coming down the lane from the main road.

'To your posts,' hissed Connolly. 'Radios on, but very low volume. And if there's only one vehicle, we take no action – we need two, and we need to catch them exchanging the stuff. Wait for the word from me ...' and we all slipped into the darkness to adopt our pre-arranged observation positions.

Due to the roughness of the track, it took the oncoming vehicle a few minutes to reach the farm buildings, but its lights swept the scene as it swung into the stable yard. There it dowsed its headlights as three men climbed out. One of them opened the door of a garage next to the stable block, and the car quickly reversed inside. All the lights went out and the door was closed by the driver, then all four disappeared into one of the looseboxes. That door was closed behind them, although the top half of the door remained open. They were now waiting as we watched them. They were awaiting vehicle No. 2.

My position was in an old implement shed among a lot of disused junk, spare parts of ploughs and harvesters, old bins and tools and so forth, but I had a fine long view of the yard. Now I could see nothing. Was that hidden car full of loot, or was it waiting to collect the loot from the other?

My heart was thumping as I waited; I found this session of observation far more exciting than Operation Phrynia, for there was going to be a dramatic and positive finale. And then came trouble.

As a second set of lights burst across the far horizon to hurtle down that road to the farm, a third set appeared from the direction of the estate entrance. Two sets of lights were therefore heading towards the farm. But there was a problem – each was flourishing a flashing blue light.

They were police cars – we were later to learn that the estate gamekeeper had seen the arrival of the first car with the men who were then in the loosebox. Suspecting them to be poachers, he had alerted the local police. And no one had told them about this operation – a selection of other operational teams had been informed, but not the local police. And so these two cars, operating very strategically, were rushing into the farm to block both exits and contain the supposed poachers and their vehicle. I knew Connolly would be tearing out his blond hair, for there was no way of halting them now. Our radio sets were not on their frequency, and our car was a long way off, in the village …

I groaned. Unless that car in the garage contained the stolen silver, the whole exercise would be wasted.

Both police cars drove into the yard, each parking so that their headlights flooded the area, and I realised that other cars would be blocking the exits at their distant points. It was a superb operation – but it was so pointless and ruinous.

Then my old colleague from Ashfordly, Sergeant Blaketon, splendid in his uniform, emerged from one of the cars. Its blue light was still flashing as other uniformed constables climbed from the second car. And then a gamekeeper appeared.

'In there,' I heard him say, as he pointed to the garage and looseboxes.

At this stage, Detective Sergeant Connolly revealed

himself to Blaketon, and so I thought I would do likewise; my two CID colleagues also appeared.

'Rhea!' cried Blaketon. 'What are you doing here … oh, and Gerry …'

'Oscar, you great oaf!' snapped Connolly. 'You've probably ruined my operation. This is a set-up. We're waiting for a cache of stolen silver to be transferred …'

Oscar Blaketon drew himself up to his full height and majesty and said, 'And I am here to catch poachers. Now Vincent,' he addressed the gamekeeper, 'where are they?'

'In that loosebox, Mr Blaketon, and their car's in yon garage …'

At this, the door of the loosebox burst open and out came three men, whose leader strode across to Blaketon.

'You rustic buffoons, you crass idiots, you utter bloody fools … you have just ruined our operation!' he snarled. 'There'll be hell to play over this. We nearly had 'em, the best tip in years, the top operators nearly trapped and you country bloody bumpkins go and blow the lot …'

'And who are you, pray?' growled Blaketon, eyeing the three scruffy individuals in their jeans and heavy sweaters.

'Regional Crime Squad, Detective Inspector Jarvis based at Durham,' and he showed his warrant card to Blaketon. 'And look what you have just done. You've just blown a major operation, you've just alerted some of the region's top villains to our plan …'

Jarvis did his nut, as the expression goes, while Blaketon, true to form, insisted he was seeking poachers and promptly took his men on a tour of the estate to find them. Gerry Connolly remained.

'If you bastards would tell us what's going on, this

wouldn't have happened ...'

'And if you woolly-backs let real detectives do their jobs, we'd have nailed this lot ...'

They argued and fought for half an hour as Blaketon and his team crunched and crashed through the woodland around the farm.

'Come on, lads,' said a depressed Connolly. 'Back to Eltering. Back to local housebreakings and petty theft. Back to minnows instead of salmon ...'

Leaving the Crime Squad to lick their wounds, we travelled back to Eltering in silence, each with his own thoughts. I felt sorry for Gerry Connolly, for, whoever his informant was, he had given superb information. As we pulled into the car park, we had to avoid a white 30-cwt van parked there. I saw it had a broken rear-light cluster.

'That's all we're good for, lads,' said Gerry, stepping out of his car, 'nicking speeders and people with duff lights on their motors!'

But inside, PC John Rogers was waiting for us with a huge smile.

'Sarge!' he said as Connolly entered. 'Thank God you've come! Traffic have stopped that van that's outside, a duff light ... it's full of silver, nicked from a job in Durham ... they've got two blokes. I was just going to give Headquarters a ring, to get them to alert the Crime Squad.'

'No need,' Gerry beamed. 'This is one for us, I think, eh lads?'

'Yes, Sarge,' we chorused as we followed him into the CID office.

Chapter 5

For when the One Great Scorer comes
To write against your name,
He marks, not that you won or lost
But how you played the game.
GRANTLAND RICE (1880-1949)

UNTIL 1968, MANY OF the crimes which involved breaking into houses and other buildings were classified by the type of premises entered in this felonious way. For example, there were schoolhouse-breaking, warehouse-breaking, Government, municipal or public building-breaking, office-breaking, counting-house-breaking, garage-breaking, factory-breaking, store-breaking and others. To break into a church or other place of divine worship to steal or to commit any other serious crime was called sacrilege, and because those places were considered the House of God, the crime was regarded as extremely serious and, until 1968, carried a maximum penalty of life imprisonment.

To break into someone's private dwelling-house was called housebreaking if it was done during the daylight hours and burglary if it was done during the night hours, i.e. between 9 p.m. and 6 a.m. Burglary was a very serious offence, and it was classified as a felony (and so was sacrilege); other felonies included crimes like murder and rape. Housebreaking, on the other hand, was considered a lesser crime because it was common law misdemeanour, although it was made into a statutory felony by the 1916 Larceny Act. Nonetheless, criminal folklore continued to ascribe it with a lesser status, and it was infinitely more desirable to have a series of housebreakings than a series of burglaries.

The difference between the two was often a matter of timing by the burglar/housebreaker. For example, if a man woke up at 7 a.m. to find his house had been broken into during the night, how could anyone prove it had been burgled? No one knew if the villains had entered before 6 a.m. – they could have got in at 6.05 a.m., and so that crime would be logged as housebreaking, not burglary. After all, no one wanted a burglary logged in their records! As a consequence of this thinking, the volume of burglaries was kept at a minimum, while housebreakings chugged along at a fairly high rate.

With the passing of the Criminal Law Act of 1967, the distinction between felonies and misdemeanours was abolished, and so these terms became obsolete – instead we had a category of crimes known as 'arrestable offences' or, more simply, just 'crimes'. And then, in 1968, the Theft Act scrapped all those old 'breaking offences', as we called them, and placed every type of breaking offence under one heading – burglary. From being a crime which had carried the death penalty for over 700 years (from around 1124 until 1838), it was now no more serious than breaking into a henhouse to steal an egg.

Older policemen were horrified, because it meant their burglary figures would soar. They could not see that the change had reduced the status of burglary instead of elevating the status of housebreaking. They couldn't see that the artificial differences between felonies and misdemeanours no longer mattered.

Another change was to call stealing 'theft' instead of larceny, and I do know these changes did alarm the elder police officers, albeit without reason.

But my period as an Aide to CID was in those halcyon days when burglaries were burglaries and felonies were felonies, and the statisticians were delighted to be able to juggle with the crime figures thus produced.

In common with most small towns, Eltering did have its outbreaks of crime. These were hardly crime waves, but they did come in identifiable types – there would be a spate of thefts from motor cars, for example, or a spate of shop-breakings, a run of thefts from public houses or a sequence of con men leaving hotels or boarding-houses without paying the bill. It was odd how these continuing crimes occurred because, quite often, a sequence of crimes was not perpetrated by the same person or gang. It almost seemed as if there were fashions for crime, fads that came and went just like any other passing craze.

But there would be outbreaks of crime that could be attributed to the same person or gang, a fact easily ascertained by the MOs of the criminals.

Such a spate involved a series of housebreakings on small estates at Eltering, but also at other small towns in the district. They had been occurring for some months and followed a similar pattern. Bungalows on small estates would be entered through ground-floor windows that had been left partially open. Country folk liked to have fresh air circulating their homes, and so they left the windows open; sensible though this might be from a health viewpoint, it is an invitation to a passing and opportunist thief or burglar. As the term 'breaking' included opening windows as well as smashing them, this series was termed 'housebreaking' because the crimes occurred during the daylight hours. The ordinary citizens, of course, did not know of these subtle categorizations, and they would report they had been burgled.

The housebreakers, to give them their official name, seemed to know when their victims were away from the premises, and a feature of their work was that they seldom caused any damage inside the houses. They rifled the premises for cash and also took valuables that were not easily identifiable, such as radio sets, binoculars, cameras, ornaments of silver and pewter and other disposable things. Cash seemed to be their main objective, however; we felt they only took those other things if cash was not quickly found. In some cases, the means of entry, through small windows high off the ground, such as toilet windows or pantry windows, suggested someone of agility and youthfulness.

Added to this was the fact that their area of operation indicated they had transport, but in every case no one had seen the villains and no one had reported a suspicious vehicle. It seemed that our crooks were invisible.

'Nick,' said Gerry Connolly one quiet morning, 'get the files on those housebreakings and go through all the reports. See if you can find any common factor we might have missed. I feel sure there's something glaringly obvious that we've overlooked. Find a quiet corner somewhere and give them your undivided attention for today.'

I enjoyed this kind of research and took all the files into the court house, which was not in use. There I began my reading and drew a chart on some lined paper; on that chart, I listed the day, date, time and estates in question, the mode of entry and all the other basic factors of each crime. I did not come to any particular conclusions, although I did discover that the earliest crime had been discovered at 11.30 a.m. and the latest at 4.30 p.m. Most had been committed on a Monday, although others had occurred on Wednesdays, Fridays and Saturdays. The victims could not be categorised either, because they included pensioners, young people, married couples, single people, rich and poor. A lot of the attacked premises were bungalows but the attacks did include semi-detached houses, terrace houses and detached properties. The majority, however, were on fairly new estates where the residents might not know all their neighbours. There, a stranger was not unusual.

I decided I would look at similar crimes in the neighbouring market towns too; while I could not obtain as much detail about them from the circulars we received, I knew I could get facts such as the dates and times, a description of the stolen goods and an idea of the kind of premises. If I needed more facts, I could obtain them from the police stations in those towns. As I worked, Gerry Connolly came in to see how I was progressing and brought me a mug of coffee; he looked at my charts and asked if I had come up with anything new, and when I said, 'No,' he smiled.

'We've tried too. Anyway, keep looking, Nick. There's nowt happening just now, so you're as well doing that. Something might click.' And he left me to my piles of paper and charts.

As I worked, nothing of note emerged until I listed the towns where the crimes had been committed together with the days when the attacks occurred.

The odd thing about Ashfordly's handful of crimes (twenty-one in the past year) was that they had all occurred on a Friday; when I checked those at Brantsford (fifteen in the year), I found they had all been committed on a Wednesday, But that did not apply to Eltering, because different days have been utilised there, and the same applied to the reported crimes at Malton. Saturday had featured prominently in Malton's tally, but so had Wednesday and Friday. Eltering's crimes had been committed on Mondays, Wednesdays, Fridays and Saturdays. There were no such crimes on Tuesdays, Thursdays and Sundays in those towns.

That seemed odd, I felt, but why? Why was it odd?

I ended that day's studies without any firm conclusions, and then the following day, Friday, I got a call from Connolly. It was half past three in the afternoon.

'Nick, there's been a housebreaking in Heather Drive, No. 18. Name of Turnbull. Cash taken. Can you attend? You'll be on your own.'

'Yes, of course.' I was a little nervous but anxious to show that I could investigate this kind of crime.

No. 18 Heather Drive was a brick-built, semi-detached bungalow on a corner site; it was on a new estate, completed only two years earlier, which occupied a sloping site on the northern edge of the town. I walked to the address and knocked; the door was opened by a solidly built man in his early sixties, and his wife stood close behind.

'Detective Constable Rhea,' I said, showing my warrant card. 'You called the office ...'

'Aye, lad, come in,' he said warmly. 'The buggers have taken our holiday savings. Now if Ah'd been here when they got in, Ah'd have skelped 'em for sure.'

'Skelped' is an old Yorkshire dialect word for 'hit'. I could well imagine this fellow tackling them and thrashing them for their cheek in invading his home.

'Where did they get in?' I asked. 'Will you show

me?'

'Pantry window,' he said, leading me through to the back of the bungalow. Mrs Turnbull followed us, wringing her hands.

'There,' he said, pointing to the window. It was only eighteen inches wide by two feet tall, but they had pushed up the bottom half from the outside and climbed through. I went outside to have a look and found they had pushed the dustbin from its position near the gate until it was beneath the window. They'd climbed upon it and had squeezed through this tiny space.

'You left the window unlocked?' I asked.

'Open,' said Mrs Turnbull. 'I allus leaves it open an inch or two, for fresh air, you see. It is a larder, you know, young man, and food needs fresh air.'

'It's sensible to screw it in position, then,' I said. 'Put screws through the frame so no one can push it further open. So they got in here, and then where did they go?'

'Into the parlour,' said Mr Turnbull, leading the way.

The parlour is what others might call the lounge. I followed the couple in. On the mantelshelf was a white vase.

'I had £85 in there,' said Mrs Turnbull. 'It's all gone.'

'In notes, was it?' I asked.

'Ten-bob notes and pound notes,' she said, 'saved up from my pension. We were going to go to Brighton, me and Lawrie.'

'I'm sorry.' I was genuinely sorry for them in their loss, and asked if anything else had been touched, or whether any other room appeared to have been searched.

None had, but I checked each one just in case.

'Now,' I said, with my notebook open, for I was recording all the necessary details, 'what about the other places you've got money hidden? People always hide

81

money all over the house, and the burglars know exactly where to look. There's no hiding place in this house that they would not find – and find easily,' I stressed. Pensioners in particular hide their spare cash instead of banking it, and it is such a simple matter for a thief to find it. I saw the looks in their eyes, and Mr Turnbull said, 'You go and look, Norma, while I pour this lad a cup of tea.'

I was not to be privy to their secret hiding places, but as I sipped tea in the kitchen, Mrs Turnbull returned smiling. 'He's nivver found any of it!' she beamed proudly. I wondered if this meant their return had disturbed the intruder, for it was odd if the intruder had not made a more thorough search of the house. I asked them to show me all around, just in case he was hiding in a wardrobe or in the loft – that was not unknown, even with a policeman in the house. But he'd gone – he'd let himself out of the front door by unlocking the Yale.

I asked if they had touched anything before ringing the police, and Mrs Turnbull said she'd 'nobbut done a bit o' dusting' to tidy the place before my arrival!

'You might have destroyed any fingerprints or other evidence,' I tried to explain. 'I'll get our fingerprints people to come and check the house – leave the pantry window.'

'He might get in again!' she snapped.

'They'll be here later today,' I said. 'And then you can secure that window – and all the others. And they'll want to examine the vase where you had the cash, and the front door – and anything else he might have touched.'

'She allus cleans up afore we have visitors,' said Mr Turnbull. 'She'll hoover again afore your fingerprint fellers get here ...'

'She'd better not!' I shook my finger at the old lady. 'Now, remember, Mrs Turnbull, don't touch anything else, not until they've done their work. It is very important that we get every scrap of evidence they might have left behind.'

'Then you'll want this!' she opened the door of the kitchen cabinet and showed me a small block of blue chalk. It was the type used by billiards and snooker-players to chalk the tips of their cues. 'Now if I hadn't hoovered before you came, I'd not have found that,' she said in some sort of triumph.

'Where was it?' I asked.

'Under t'sofa,' she beamed. 'Now it's not mine and it's not our Lawrie's, and it wasn't there when I hoovered up yesterday, and it wasn't there when I hoovered up this morning before we went off to Ashfordly market. So he must have dropped it.'

Her logic was impeccable, so I pocketed the chalk. It could be relevant. The snag was it was one of millions of such cubes – it would prove very little even if we found the owner. But it *was* of value. Every clue left at the scene of a crime is of some value, however limited.

I took particulars of all the necessary details, said we would investigate the crime and reassured them that our fingerprint experts would arrive later in the day. And then, as I walked back to the police station, I realised that Mrs Turnbull had said something highly significant.

After completing my crime report, I went to the files I'd been using the day before. Market day! Market day in Ashfordly was a Friday – and its recent housebreakings had been committed on Fridays; market day in Brantsford was a Wednesday, and its breakings were on Wednesdays. That pattern did not fit Eltering or Malton – but Eltering's market day was Monday, and a lot of its breakings had been on Mondays, while many of Malton's had been Saturdays – its market day. And then I realised that Eltering's and Malton's other breakings had been committed during market days at Ashfordly and Brantsford.

So either the villains were stopping off at Eltering and Malton on their way home to commit further crimes or they had found a way of knowing when folks were out of their homes, attending those other markets ...

I was excited about this and was making notes when Gerry Connolly came in.

'Well, Nick, how did it go?'

I explained what had happened at the Turnbulls' home and before I could tell him about the cue chalk, he asked a few pertinent questions, then he said, 'Well, while you were out, there was a development. A minor one, but it could be important. I've been talking to D/S Miller at Scarborough; they've got a pair of suspects for us, names of two local lads who've been selling stuff to second-hand dealers and junk shops in Scarborough. They've a van which they rig up to look like a window-cleaner's vehicle with a ladder on top, and they've been spending freely lately – but not cleaning many windows. Miller says they spend their days in the snooker hall. I thought we might give them an unannounced call.'

'Then this will interest you,' I said, picking up the chalk which I had now placed in an envelope, labelled with the crime report number.

'Bloody hell!' he beamed. 'It's amazing how things come together ... right, tomorrow then? You and I will go to Scarborough.'

'It's a Saturday,' I said. 'They might come out to Malton to do a job.'

'Then I'll give Malton police their vehicle number

and we can keep our eyes open for them. But we'll do that snooker hall anyway, in the evening.'

And so we did. There was no reported housebreaking in Malton that Saturday, and we arrived at the snooker hall at six o'clock.

Gerry booked a table and we had a game of snooker; he thrashed me soundly and I said, 'You've played this game before!'

'Once or twice,' he smiled. 'Ah, these are our men,' and two men in their early twenties came to one of the tables. Before they began to play, Connolly went across.

'Got a bit of chalk I can borrow, lads?' he asked, holding his cue.

'Sure, mate,' and one of them pulled a piece from his pocket. It bore the same blue paper covering as the one I'd recovered at the Turnbulls'.

'You are Terry Leedham and Graham Scott,' he smiled charmingly at them.

'So what if we are?' responded Leedham.

'I'm Detective Sergeant Connolly from Eltering, and this is D/PC Rhea. We're investigating a series of housebreakings in the area, and think you lads might help us with our enquiries. In fact, we've brought some of your chalk back – you left it in one of the houses you raided.'

And he produced my bit of chalk, still in its envelope marked officially with the crime reference. It was clear from the expressions on their faces that they were the guilty parties, but every police officer knows that knowledge of guilt is not proof of guilt. I could see that they wondered how much we really knew. In fact, we knew nothing that would prove a case against them – we had no fingerprints, nothing.

It was just supposition and so we needed a cough, as

the CID term an admission.

'We know you're the culprits,' said Connolly, 'and we can prove it ...'

They looked at each other in amazement at this sudden confrontation, then Scott said, 'You'll get nowt from us, mate. No coughs, no admissions, you'll have to prove your case all the way, every inch ...'

'You are sporting lads,' he smiled again. 'You like a game of snooker?'

'Yeh, course we do. We practically live 'ere.'

'I'll take the pair of you on,' offered Connolly. 'Me against the two of you. If I win, you admit those crimes, you give us a cough to save us proving the case, If you win, you don't need to give us a cough – but we'll go off and prove you've done those jobs – and mebbe lots more.'

'Gerraway, that's stupid!' laughed Scott.

'No,' said Leedham. 'We can beat a cop any day, Graham; that'll get him off our backs.'

I could see that Leedham was anxious to take on this challenge, and then, as I glanced around the walls of the hall, I knew why. He was a club champion, a winner of several trophies. I tried to warn Connolly but was too late because he said, 'Right. It's on, is it?'

'Best of three frames?' chuckled Leedham. 'Tell you what, this is the easiest interrogation I've ever had ...'

Scott was not so willing, but he could not let his partner down and so the game was on, with Gerry Connolly playing each in turn, their scores counting as one man's. I acted as marker. It is not necessary to go into the details of that game, except to say that Gerry Connolly trounced them. He won the first two games and insisted they play the third – which he also won.

'Right, lads, time to cough those jobs, eh?' he said.

And to my surprise, Leedham agreed. He sat down with Connolly and admitted a string of housebreakings, with Connolly showing him a list of outstanding ones in Malton, Eltering, Ashfordly and Brantsford. Scott joined in too – he had no alternative. It was a most surprising gesture by these two criminals.

'What made you make that weird offer?' I put to Connolly in the car after the pair had been bailed at Scarborough Police Station.

'I was relying on a bit of gen I got from the local lads,' he said. 'They said Leedham was a superb snooker-player, a real talent, but he couldn't afford to go professional. He wasn't in work, so he couldn't pay his way in most amateur games. He took to crime to help him continue playing – and they say he's the most honest of sportsmen, he'll never cheat in a game. A curious mixture – so I issued that challenge.'

'You could have lost,' I said.

'I could,' he smiled, 'But I didn't.'

I was to learn soon afterwards that Gerry Connolly had been the National Police Snooker Champion for five successive years and runner-up on no fewer than three other occasions. He'd also won many contests outside the police service.

(*Author's note:* Some seventeen years after this incident, I found myself breakfasting at a police training centre with the then Director of Public Prosecutions. I told him of this strange case and asked him whether, in his opinion, such a confession would be admissible in court had it been challenged by the defence. He expressed an opinion that it would be admissible because it had been freely given without any duress.)

If the actions of Terry Leedham were surprising, those of a lady, the victim of a housebreaking, were touching. She rang the police station to report the theft, for someone had sneaked into her home during the morning and had stolen several items. I was sent to investigate.

'Well, Mrs Harland,' I said as she showed me into her parlour, 'what can you tell me?'

'Ah nobbut popped out for a minute.' She was a lady in her sixties, the widow of a retired farmer. 'Round to t'corner shop for some flour and lard. Ah mean, Mr Rhea, up on t'moors, there's neea need ti lock doors or owt, is there, and folks nivver come pinching.'

'That's true,' I agreed. 'But this is a town, you know, and you should lock your doors, even if you're out only for a moment or two. Now, what's been taken?'

'My housekeeping. I keep it in yon box on t'mantelshelf. Nobbut £8 and a few coppers. A pair o' brass candlesticks from t'piano top, a silver mug that my dad left me when he died, and three black cats, ebony they are. Now, they're t'worst loss, Mr Rhea, a family heirloom, they are, very old. They were my grandmother's; she worked for Queen Victoria at Buckingham Palace, as a cook, and the Queen gave her those cats. They've come right down through t'family, daughter by daughter. Not worth a lot, mind, but, well, I'm right saddened about them being taken.'

She gave me a cup of tea and a scone as I took descriptions of all the missing objects, and I assured her that details would be circulated among the local second-hand and antique dealers. The value of the missing items was low, and I could not understand why anyone had stolen them – it seemed to be the work of an opportunist thief who had taken the cash and anything else that might make a few shillings.

The three cats seemed to be the most interesting –

they were each carved from ebony and, according to Mrs Harland, they had green eyes 'that shone a bit' and 'claws made oot o' gold-coloured stuff', and each wore a leather collar studded 'wi' bits o' red glass'.

Each was in a sitting position, one being six inches or so in height, one about four inches and a kitten about 2½ inches high. They were linked together with a gold-coloured chain which was threaded through their collars. Without seeing these objects, I had to rely on her description of them, but I did wonder if, in fact, those 'green eyes that shone a bit', the 'bits o' gold-coloured stuff' on their claws and the 'red glass' on their collars were genuine gold and real jewels. Mrs Harland could not put a financial value on the cats and so, for the record, I recorded them as being worth £10 for the set. In our reports, we had to show the financial value of stolen goods.

Sergeant Connolly said I should tour the second-hand shops in town and other places that might sell the stolen goods, and so I did. But no one had been offered them. After those initial enquiries, there was little more that could be done, for new crimes were being recorded and investigated and the theft from Mrs Harland looked like being just another undetected crime.

It would be a month later when I received a second call from Mrs Harland.

'Mr Rhea!' she shouted into the telephone in the manner of one unaccustomed to using such new-fangled inventions. 'Them cats o' mine, Ah've come across 'em.'

For the briefest of moments, I could not recall the cats about which she spoke, and then, just in time, I remembered.

'Have you?' I said. 'Whereabouts?'

'In a house window ledge, up Curnow Street, No. 3. Ah've made a note o' t'number.'

'Can you be sure they're yours?' I would have to exercise enormous discretion if I was virtually to accuse a householder of stealing them; they could be identical, or very similar, copies.

'Aye,' she sounded hurt. ''Course Ah can; yan on 'em has a claw missing, middle cat, left back leg.'

'I'll go and ask about them,' I assured her. 'I'll come back and let you know how I go on.'

'So long as I get my cats back, that's all Ah want,' and she slammed down the telephone.

I told Sergeant Connolly, and he felt she could be mistaken, but I remembered the incident of my own stolen coat. I knew my own coat, just as Mrs Harland most surely know her own cats, cats that were part of her family history. Connolly listened to my arguments on her behalf and said, 'Fine, right. Go and sort it out, Nick. But for God's sake be careful. We don't want folks complaining that we're accusing them of housebreaking and theft.'

I knew the dangers, and it was with some trepidation, therefore, that I walked to Curnow Street to sort out this dilemma.

Curnow Street comprised semi-detached and detached houses with large-paned windows overlooking tiny gardens which abutted the street. No.3 was a pleasant, brick-built semi with pretty curtains at its window. As I approached, I saw no cats sitting there. I wondered how I would tackle the delicate accusation I was duty bound to make. But my immediate worries were solved. As I was about to walk up the short path to the front door, someone opened it. A young woman in her early thirties, with a pretty face atop a rather heavily built body, was trying to manoeuvre from the house a wheelchair containing a large child. The child was a girl of about twelve with long, dark brown hair and sad eyes, and a rug covered her lower regions and legs. The plump young woman was battling to lower the chair down two steps and, at the same time, keep the heavy door from slamming shut. I went to help her.

'Thanks.' She clearly welcomed the extra pair of hands, and I coaxed the heavy chair down the steps and onto the path. And then I saw the three cats; they were laid on the lap of the girl, on top of the all-embracing blanket. I had to make use of this heaven-sent opportunity, so I picked up the cats and tried to make contact with the girl. But she was a spastic, I felt, and communication was not easy.

'They're nice,' I said, half to the girl and half to the woman, whom I assumed was her mother.

'They're Eve's,' I was told. 'She loves cats and we had a big black one, but she got knocked down by a bus a couple of weeks ago. She had kittens once, a year or two ago, but they died. Eve was heart-broken.'

Eve tried to speak to me about those model cats but I could not understand her. I wished I could communicate with her, for her hands were moving around in her attempt to speak. I replaced the cats in her lap, having seen that they corresponded in every detail to those stolen from Mrs Harland.

'They're lovely cats, Eve,' I said gently.

'I found them on a bric-à-brac stall in the market last Monday,' said the mother. 'Eve was with me and I knew she wanted them, so I got them. They were only £3, a real bargain.'

'They look like ebony,' I said.

'The man on the stall thought that too,' she said. 'He

thought they'd been carved in Africa or India.'

I did not tell this lady, whose name I learned was Mrs Ann Reynolds, of the real reason for my visit. I allowed her to think I just happened to be passing, and I did not tell her I was a policeman; I felt a twinge of guilt at my deception but felt, in the circumstances, it was justified.

It was Monday that day, so I went to the market and found the bric-à-brac stall. It was there every Monday.

'You had some black cats here last week,' I said, without saying who I was. 'Three of them, ebony I think, linked with a gold chain.'

'Sold,' he said. 'A little lass in a wheelchair wanted them, so I let her have 'em cheap.'

'Can I ask where you got them?' I put to him.

'You the police, then?' he put to me.

'CID,' I said. 'We've had a report of some cats like that being stolen locally.'

'A feller came to me only last Monday morning with 'em,' he said. 'Scruffy chap, two or three days' growth of whiskers, bit a down-and-outer, I'd say. He sold 'em to me, said they were his. I mean, Officer, I don't deal in knocked-off stuff, never have. Mind, I do get offered stuff that sometimes I wonder about, and if I'm worried, I leave it alone. But them cats, well, they're the sort of thing you can pick up in any souvenir shop.'

I disagreed with his assessment of their merits but did not argue with him. I believed his story and made a note of his description of the man who had sold the cats. I did not feel that this man knew he had bought stolen goods, and he was not therefore culpable, but he would have to feature in my crime report. However, who was the rightful owner of the cats, assuming they were the ones stolen from Mrs Harland?

She must inspect them and identify them as her

property before any further legal proceedings could be taken. I knew I should have taken possession of those cats until the matter was determined, but I had shrunk from that action, rightly or wrongly. Mrs Harland, the loser, did have an obvious claim to the cats, but so did Mrs Reynolds, who had purchased them in good faith. If a battle over ownership did result, it was not the duty of the police to sort it out. That rested first upon the respective claimants and, if they could not agree, recourse through the civil courts was available – they would determine true ownership. But that was a last resort. In the event of a criminal prosecution of the thief, a court could order the return of the cats to Mrs Harland, and possibly some compensation to Mrs Reynolds. But first we had to catch the thief – his description would be circulated. In the meantime, I decided to pay a visit to Mrs Harland to acquaint her with the day's odd circumstances.

She welcomed me and I knew, by the expression on her face, that she had expected me to be clutching her three cats upon arrival. She took me into the parlour, produced a cup of tea within seconds, plus a buttered scone and some strawberry jam, and said, 'Well now, Mr Rhea, so you've not found my cats.'

'On the contrary,' I said, and I launched into the story of my enquiries, and of Eve's role in all this. Mrs Harland listened intently and I concluded by saying, 'What you must do now, Mrs Harland, is accompany me to the Reynolds' home to identify those cats formally. If they are yours, we can then take charge of them until the ownership has been determined or until the thief is arrested and dealt with.'

'Now that's a rum 'un,' she said, and she fell into a long silence which I did not interrupt. I wondered what she was thinking.

Then she brightened up and said, 'Mr Rhea, Ah'd like yon little lass to keep 'em. I've no daughter to pass 'em on to, no son either, and yon invalid lass is welcome to 'em. She has no idea they were stolen, has she?'

'No,' I said. 'Her mother bought them in good faith from the market. She has no idea where they came from before that.'

I now realised I had problems of my own, for the writing-off of this reported crime would create some administrative problems. I started to explain the difficulties to Mrs Harland but she was equal to the occasion.

'The way Ah sees it,' she smiled, 'is that Ah was mistaken when Ah spotted them cats in yon window. Ah've had a closer look, and they're not mine. Similar, mebbe, but definitely not mine.'

'That would keep the books straight, Mrs Harland.' I had to admire her decision.

'And it'll keep a little lass very happy, eh?'

'It will,' I said. 'Thank you.'

And as I left, I recalled the old Yorkshire belief that, if a black cat enters a house, it is a sign of good luck. I hoped three ebony ones would bring a spot of good fortune and happiness to little Eve Reynolds and her family.

Chapter 6

Death, in itself, is nothing.
JOHN DRYDEN (1631-1700)

IN POLICE CIRCLES, THE quotation from John Dryden given above is very true. Police officers deal with death in all its forms, and it is surprising just what a large part this most unavoidable of natural states plays in their daily work. Murders, manslaughters, infanticides, homicides in all their mystery and cruelty, suicides, sudden deaths, deaths from unknown causes, deaths in mysterious circumstances, accidents with motor vehicles, firearms or other devices, drownings, poisonings and druggings, falling off cliffs or down mine shafts, leaping off bridges or out of aircraft, and a whole host of other curious forms of leaving this earthly life are the lot of the constable on duty. A straightforward natural death, where someone simply drifts cheerfully into the hereafter, is therefore of little consequence, a matter only for doctors, clergymen and undertakers, plus, of course, the friends and family of the dear departed.

On many occasions, however, the distinction between a natural death and a suspicious one is not easy to determine. Complications arise, sometimes due to the place in which the demise occurred, sometimes due to the curious manner in which the departure from life took place. In such cases, the police do have a duty to examine the circumstances and to involve others –

coroners, forensic experts, doctors and pathologists – in an attempt to determine whether or not foul play is suspected.

Being involved in an enquiry into a mysterious death is truly fascinating, and most officers, when undergoing their basic training, are advised that their manner of investigating these deaths is a fine introduction to CID work. It is also a wonderful way of performing a service to the public, because a considerate but efficient investigator, when working so closely with the bereaved relatives or friends, can rapidly enhance the stature of himself and the entire police service. I have known very determined anti-police citizens revise their opinions of the force as a direct result of being involved in such an enquiry, especially when it was conducted by a sensitive and efficient constable.

In most parts of the country, the investigation of a sudden or mysterious death is the responsibility of the officer to whom the report is made, as a consequence of which many uniformed constables find themselves engaged in this work. In other areas, particularly in urban communities, a constable is appointed to the post of Coroner's Officer and undertakes all such routine enquiries. It demands a special kind of sympathy and understanding of human nature to cope with sudden death every day of one's working life, but these officers perform their duties in a cheerful and professional manner.

There are times when the police officer is the only friend the family has in their loss, the only one to offer help without complications.

The CID are called in only when the suspicious death is confirmed as being truly worthy of their interest as a possible homicide. At Eltering, because it was a small town, the CID took an interest in most suspicious deaths (as in Chapter 2), even though there was little likelihood of their being a homicide. Nonetheless, one or two further intriguing cases of death came my way during those few weeks as an Aide to CID.

One such example occurred on a Saturday morning, and it illustrated the curious way that some people have of behaving in the face of events which are outside the normal scope of their work and daily routine. As a result of this case, and the one which follows, I realised that there are people who simply cannot cope with the dramatic, unusual or unexpected; they categorically will not accept any responsibility over and above that which their job entails. To avoid such pressures, they simply behave as if the dramatic, unusual or unexpected has never occurred. There are times when I think this would make a fascinating matter for research, to show how a human being can avoid coping with something that is presented before his or her very eyes.

This trend often manifests itself during a crisis in the streets or other public places – passers-by simply ignore what is happening and walk on, even if someone is dying or being raped or mugged. I have often wondered how such passers-by can live with their consciences, knowing that their immediate action, had they done something, could have saved a life or prevented a crime, even if that action required nothing more than making a fuss or ringing 999. But so many citizens refrain from 'getting involved', as they term it – they do absolutely nothing. Police officers cannot behave like this. However terrified and uncertain they are, however young and inexperienced, they must cope with everything from lost dogs to exploding bombs via crashed aircraft, crimes, dramas of every kind, whether large or small, and, of course, sudden or unexplained deaths.

The case which follows is a fine illustration of this tendency, and it started with a telephone call from an estate agent.

'My name is Walters,' he told the duty constable, PC John Rogers. 'I'm employed by Pendle Smith and Watson, estate agents. I have just found a dead man in a house we are selling. The house is empty by the way ...'

The only uniform constable on duty in Eltering that morning was dealing with a traffic accident at the roundabout in the High Street, and so Gerry Connolly suggested I went along, 'Just to have a look and see if he's not imagining things.' I said I would be pleased to do so, and off I went.

The house was a pretty terrace cottage, No. 14 High Forest Terrace in Eltering, a loftily situated row of stone-built houses overlooking Low Forest Terrace. I arrived within five minutes to find a worried-looking individual on the doorstep. He was a small, mild-mannered man with thinning dark hair and he clutched a briefcase to his chest.

'I'm D/PC Rhea,' I introduced myself. 'Are you Mr Walters?'

'I am, yes, and this is terrible, Mr Rhea, it really is. I mean, fancy coming to check a house over and finding a corpse ...'

'Show me,' I asked him.

The body was that of a late-middle-aged man, probably in his mid-sixties, and it was fully dressed in grey trousers, a blue shirt, grey pullover and black shoes; the unfortunate fellow was lying on the bare floorboards of the main bedroom of this empty two-bedroomed property. I touched the corpse on the cheek; it was stone cold, and rigor mortis had set in; he was dead all right.

This man had died in a sleeping position, for he was laid out as if he was still in the Land of Nod, and his corpse was as stiff as the proverbial board. I could see no sign of visible injury but would have to strip him at the mortuary to check those parts of his body that were clothed. That was one of the jobs of an investigating officer – in this case, me.

There was the smell of death in the air as, with Walters following me around, I did a quick survey of the windows and doors to see if there had been any forcible entry. This death was certainly suspicious – after all, what explanation could there be for it?

'Who is he? Any idea?' I asked.

'Sorry, no. I'm new, I didn't handle the sale of this house, you see; one of my colleagues did. He's gone off on holiday, to Tenerife; he did the sale, you see, and I was just checking that the outgoing owner had cleared his furnishings, a courtesy, you know, towards the incoming owners ... we make a practice of checks of this kind before we let the new purchasers in. They're due very soon – today, in fact.'

'So you are saying this house has been sold?' I asked.

'Yes, completion is today. The owner is a Mr ... er ...' and he examined his files. 'Er ... Mr ... Clough, Mr Martin Clough, yes. Well, he had to be out today and our new owners are moving in this afternoon. This is rather, er, well unexpected ... embarrassing ... To be honest, Officer, I do not know what to do ...'

'They won't be too happy about having a body on the floor, will they?' I said. 'So who is this dead man? Is it Mr Clough?'

' 'Well, er, I don't know. I haven't met him, you see.'

'If it is Mr Clough, where is all his furniture?' I put to the estate agent.

'Well, that's a puzzle as well, isn't it? I mean, so far as I know, the removal men were due this morning ... maybe they've been, maybe Mr Clough came back for something and died ...'

'Was the house locked up when you arrived?' I asked.

'Oh, yes, but we have a spare key.'

'And where will the other key be, assuming it is not lying in this poor fellow's pockets?'

'I expect the removal men will have used it. They'll bring it to the office in due course ... They sometimes get it from the outgoing owner and lock up after themselves ... We ask them to take charge of the keys, you see. We don't like outgoing owners keeping them ... for security, you know. Some have been known to let themselves back in to collect things they thought the removal men had left behind ... very thoughtless ... illegal anyway ...'

'Who are the removal men?' I asked in an effort to stop his waffling.

'Lapsley and Power,' he said. 'From York.'

'And where was the furniture going?'

'To York, to a bungalow Mr Clough had bought – through us, I might add.'

'Well, Mr Walters, this chap is as dead as a dodo, and the smell's going to get worse before too long, so we'd better get him shifted, hadn't we?'

'Er, well, yes, I suppose so. Do you want me to give you a lift with him?'

'Thanks, but no. There are things to do first. I'll have to get a doctor in to certify death, and if possible to state the cause of death. And then we'll see about getting this chap moved somewhere. Where can we put him, Mr Walters? We can hardly stand him in a corner to look lively, can we? Or pretend he's the gasman who's come

100

to check the fittings. He's about as lively as some officials I've come across. And we can't have him littering the floor when folks want to put the carpets down, can we?'

'Er, no, well, I suppose not.' By now, poor Mr Walters was very worried and kept referring to his watch.

Leaving him with the corpse, I went to the cottage next door and spoke to a lady. Yes, she knew Mr Clough very well, and her description fitted the man upstairs. I did not ask her to come and look at him; I felt we could identify him quite easily by other means, perhaps via his doctor. The neighbour said his medical practitioner was Dr Craven of Eltering, and she added that the old man had been under treatment for some weeks. I returned to Clough's cottage and used the telephone, which had not been cut off, to call Dr Craven. Fortunately he was available and would come immediately. We waited, with me puzzling about Mr Clough's furniture, and the unhappy Mr Walters worrying if his new owners would arrive to find the corpse still in their bedroom.

I wondered what the legal situation was if the owner of a property remained on the premises after completion of the purchase, albeit in the form of a corpse. Could a corpse be a trespasser? Certainly he could not be prosecuted, but could his relatives be held responsible for his refusal to move out at the correct time? Was there any negligence here? It was an area of civil law that did not come within the scope of police work, fortunately.

During my musings, Dr Craven arrived. He examined the corpse, said it was Mr Clough and announced he was prepared to certify the death as being of natural causes, a heart failure, he affirmed. He'd been treating Mr Clough for heart problems, and he could make the formal identification that we required. The old man was a widower with no family, but he had relations in York.

This matter settled, I rang Eltering Police Office and asked for the shell to be driven around in the van – the shell was a plastic coffin which we used for moving bodies. The van arrived, driven by PC Gregory, and I helped him to lift the remains of Mr Clough into the shell. We replaced the lid and as our van, with Mr Clough on board, turned away from the premises, I saw the approach of a small green Ford Anglia containing a man and woman.

'Oh, dear, here they are ...' said Mr Walters. 'I do hope nothing will be said. We don't want a back word to be given at this stage, good heavens no ...'

'Mum's the word,' I said. 'But I'd open the windows if I were you, Mr Walters, to let some fresh air in. He was starting to get a bit ripe. You could always blame someone's dirty socks, I suppose. Well, I'll be off now.'

I left the house and walked back to the police station, knowing we would have to trace Mr Clough's relations in order to arrange a funeral. They would probably be waiting at his new house with the kettle on, and I would ask a York police officer to call there with the sad news, but fortunately, as his death was due to natural causes, there would be no post-mortem and no inquest.

But where was the furniture from the house, and how did poor old Clough come to be lying on the bare floor? I rang the removal firm, Lapsley & Power, and asked if the men who had removed his furniture had returned. I was told, 'No, they're still unloading at York.'

It was estimated they would return to base around 7 p.m., and so I decided I must interview them. At 7 p.m. I drove to their office and waited. They were fairly prompt, because they pulled their pantechnicon into the yard at ten past seven. They garaged the huge lorry and went into the office to book off, and so I walked in behind them. They were a pair of men in their forties, each about five feet six inches tall and rather solidly built. They were like Tweedledum and Tweedledee, I thought, one sporting a bushy black moustache and the other having his untidy hair long, straggly and probably unwashed.

'Now then,' I said, 'I'm D/PC Rhea from Eltering. Can I have a brief word?'

'We're supposed to finish at seven,' said Tweedledum.

'We're working over now,' said Tweedledee. 'The boss doesn't like paying overtime, 'specially on Saturdays ...'

'It won't take a minute.' I stood before them as they both stared at me. 'Now, did you shift the furniture from High Forest Terrace today? A Mr Clough's house?'

'We did. 14 High Forest Terrace to 27 Henson Green Lane, York. Full house contents. Here, this is the key to the Clough job. We leave it here,' and Tweedledum plonked it in a tray on the desk, clearly proud of his firm's system for such things.

'Did you come across anything odd at Clough's house?'

They looked at each other, frowning, and then Tweedledee said, 'No, nowt really. No winding staircase. No narrow passages. No trouble at all, no wardrobe that wouldn't come downstairs, no iron-framed pianos, no fish-tanks full of guppies. No carpets nailed down. No, no problems. It was an ordinary job, really. Cheap stuff, most of it. Nowt very good, I'd say, no mirrors or marble washstands worth smashing ...'

I found this an odd interview, to say the least, for I

was sure the body must have been there as they worked. I knew I must ask the direct question.

'And Mr Clough? Was he there?'

'There was a chap there, yes.'

'Where was he? What was he doing?' I asked.

Tweedledum responded. 'He was upstairs on t'bed. Dead, I reckon. We tried to rouse him, but he wouldn't have any of it, so we thought he must have passed away.'

'So what did you do?' I asked.

'Laid him on t'floor while we shifted his bed. Rolled him over to shift the mat we'd put him on, and left him there. He'd got the stuff ready, mind, pots and pans packed in boxes, ornaments in tea-chests and such like. He'd done a fair job of packing; that's what I said at the time, didn't I? Many younger folks would have done a lot worse ... some can't pack for toffee ... anyroad, it wasn't a long job, not as it would have been if we'd had to pack right from the start.'

'Didn't you tell anybody – about Mr Clough, I mean?'

They looked at one another as if this was a stupid question. 'Nay, lad, that was nowt to do with us.' Tweedledee acted as spokesman now. 'We were there to shift furniture, not to do t'undertaker's job. T'only problem was finding somewhere to put him while we demolished his bed, but he was no trouble really. We got finished on time.'

'But don't you think you should have called the doctor or someone?'

'He was dead. There was nowt a doctor could do,' said Tweedledee. 'Besides, our boss says we've not to get involved in things that don't concern us. Our job is to shift furniture and to make sure it's shifted on time, with no overtime. Very particular is our boss about suchlike.'

Tweedledum then added his wisdom: 'If we did all t'things folks ask us while we're moving stuff, we'd never be finished. One woman wanted us to help paper t'ceiling, and a feller once asked if I'd help him fix his leaking toilet basin ... so our boss says never do other folk's jobs. See to your own, he says ... so shifting bodies is not our job, Mr Rhea. That's for t'undertaker, so we didn't get involved. We had a timetable to keep, you see, and there's no time to go chasing folks and ordering coffins and things when you've got to get loaded up and unpacked in t'same day.'

I took a statement from them and was satisfied in my own mind that poor old Mr Clough had packed his belongings the previous night and afterwards had simply passed away on his bed. He had not locked up that night, and these characters had simply let themselves in that morning to go about their work. And so they had, without letting a dead body interrupt their tight timetable.

I left them. I was amazed that they could ignore such a thing, and I wondered if they'd claim overtime from their boss for the time they spent with me.

I also wondered what they would have done if Mr Clough had been lying there in his coffin with the lid shut. I reckon they'd have moved him to his new house in York.

If the behaviour of those removal men seems bizarre, I can support it with a similar tale from a village on the moors.

I was working one Thursday morning at Eltering Police Station when a call came from a hiker. He was ringing from a telephone kiosk at Briggsby and sounded panic-stricken. I happened to be near the phone in the

105

police station when it rang, and as PC Rogers was dealing with a motorist at the counter, I answered.

'Eltering Police,' I said.

'Hello?' the voice sounded full of anxiety. 'Hello? Oh, is that the police?'

'Detective PC Rhea speaking,' I said slowly.

'Oh, thank God for that! Look, I'm ringing from a kiosk at Briggsby. You know it?'

'I do,' I said, for it was on my own rural beat.

'There's a body in the church,' he gasped. 'Dead ...'

'Maybe there's going to be a funeral,' I tried to soothe him. 'Bodies are taken into church before the funeral ...'

'In coffins, yes, but this one is lying on one of the pews. Near the front. He's got a notice on him saying, "Pray for the soul of Mr Aiden Bradley".'

'Is it a joke of some kind?' I asked. 'Is someone playing a joke on you?'

'Look, Officer, I know a dead body when I see one. I'm a tutor in first aid, and I am a responsible person. If you want to check, my name is Welham, George Welham, and I live at Moorways, Albion Road, Middlesbrough.'

'Point taken, Mr Welham. I'll come straight away. Will you wait? I'll be there in twenty minutes.'

I told John Rogers where I was going and what the call had alleged, and he chuckled. He thought it was some kind of village prank, a joke against the verger or the vicar, but logged it in our occurrence book.

I drove out to Briggsby, a pretty community high on the moors. It comprises a handful of cottages, one or two farms and a tiny parish church which perches on a small patch of rising ground. I eased to a halt outside and saw a man, in full hiking gear, waiting for me. His rucksack

106

stood on the wall of the graveyard. I could see the relief in his face as I stepped from the car. I introduced myself.

'This is a most unlikely story,' I said. 'Sorry if I sounded full of disbelief ...'

'I think I'd have done the same!' he smiled. 'I've been back inside once or twice, just to convince myself, but he's still there. He *is* dead, Officer; he is not pretending; he is not asleep, and I don't think the notice is a joke of any sort.'

George Welham was a tall, slim man in his thirties; he wore heavy hiking boots, thick tweed trousers and a warm red sweater.

'Show me,' I invited.

He led me into the dim interior and we walked in silence towards the altar. At the front of the pews, he halted and pointed to the first pew on the left.

And there, as he had stated, was the body of an elderly man. He was fully clothed in a dark suit and was lying on the pew with his feet towards the aisle. His hands were crossed upon his chest. The solid backrest of the pew shielded him from view, and even when one was sitting in the second pew, he was almost out of sight; I wondered how long he had been here. A congregation could assemble without realizing he was lying here, unless anyone wanted to sit beside him. He could have been here for ages ... but I felt not. Decomposition had not yet set in, although he was exuding a bit of a pong. As Welham had mentioned on the telephone, there was a handwritten notice on his chest, held secure beneath his hands, and it read, 'Pray for the soul of Mr Aiden Bradley.'

I felt his hands and face; he was cold, and rigor mortis had set in. He was as dead as the proverbial dodo. I asked Mr Welham a few pertinent questions, such as the time he had found him, whether he had moved him or called a doctor. He had done neither, and I then allowed him to leave. The problem of Mr Aiden Bradley was now mine. I searched his pockets for something by which to confirm his likely identity but, apart from a few coins, a comb and a handkerchief, there was nothing.

There were the usual formalities to arrange, such as certification of death, but how had the man come to be here and who had placed the notice on his chest? I did not know Mr Bradley and felt he was not a local man.

I decided to visit the adjoining farm to begin my enquiries, and to use their telephone to call a doctor and to arrange for the shell to be brought from Eltering.

'Bradley?' responded Joe Crawford, the farmer who lived next door to the church. 'Nivver 'eard of 'im. He's not a local, I'll tell thoo that for nowt.'

'You've no vicar here, have you?' I asked.

'Nay, lad, he comes in fre' Crampton. Covers Crampton, Briggsby and Gelderslack parishes. 'E lives in Crampton.'

'Thanks, I'll have a word with him. Does anybody in the village have a key for the church?'

'Aye, awd Mrs Dodson at Forge Cottage. She's t'cleaner.'

I explained the problem, but it didn't seem to worry Joe Crawford; as he said, 'Yon choch 'as a few bodies in it ivvery year, Mr Rhea, so another 'un isn't owt to shout about.'

I called Dr McGee, who had to travel from Elsinby, and in the meantime I went to see awd Mrs Dodson. She was a lady in her eighties who had been church cleaner for more than sixty years.

'I'd like to borrow your key for the church.' I spoke loudly, noticing the hearing-aid unit strapped to her belt. 'I might have to lock it until we've investigated a matter.'

'Summat wrang, is there?' she shouted at me.

'There's a dead man in church.' I knew I would have trouble explaining the matter in detail. 'We might have to seal the church until we've investigated his death.'

'I hope he hasn't made a mess,' she bellowed. 'I swept out last week. I should 'ave been in this morning, but my brush head fell off.'

'It's a Mr Bradley, I think,' I told her.

'He rents that cottage at the end of Green Lane.' The words rang in my ears. 'He comes for weekends and holidays.'

That explained why I did not know him.

'Where from?' I asked. 'Do you know? Has he any family?'

'Bradford,' she said. 'He's a retired wool merchant. I clean for him, an' all. After I do the church, I do his cottage, but my brush head's fallen off ...'

'I'll fix it,' I said.

She brought it to me, together with a hammer and a box of nails, and I set about securing the brush head to the shaft. As I hammered in the nail, she said, 'Ah've had yon brush for thirty-five years, and all Ah've had for it is three new heads and two new shafts.'

'Really?' I wondered if this was a kind of joke, but she sounded serious and proud of her brush.

'Brushes were made to last in them days.' she beamed.

'Did you go to the church this morning?' I asked her as I finished hammering the nail through the hole in the head.

'No,' she hollered. 'Thursdays is my day, but because that head fell off ...'

'So who would go in this morning?'

'The vicar,' she boomed. 'He has his own key. He has a service on Thursday mornings, ten o'clock. Not many folks go, mind, not like they used to. Mr Bradley allus went if he was staying here ...'

'I'll wait at the church for the doctor,' I told her. 'And then I'll take Mr Bradley away to the mortuary. If anybody comes asking about him, relations mebbe, tell them to get in touch with me at Eltering Police Station. Rhea is the name. Then I'll lock the church and bring you the key; don't unlock it until I tell you. I'll probably ring later today, when we know whether this is a suspicious death.'

'222,' she barked. 'My number.'

'Thanks,' and I left with the key in my hand.

'Bye, Mr Rhea,' she thundered as I made my way back to the church.

Dr Archie McGee, smelling of whisky in spite of the hour, arrived and I showed him the corpse.

'Dead,' he said. 'Very dead, Nick, old son. I'll certify that but I cannot certify the cause. He was not my patient; never seen the follow before.'

So that meant a post-mortem. However, I thanked him and off he went. The van containing the shell arrived shortly afterwards, and we loaded Mr Bradley, complete with his request to God, and sent him on his way to the mortuary. Later I would ask Bradford police to trace his relatives and hoped his cottage would reveal an address at which we could begin; that had to be searched next. I did find an address in his bedroom at the cottage and would relay that to Bradford for enquiries to be made.

My immediate job now was to find the vicar. I drove to his small, modern vicarage at Crampton and found him in the garden tending a border. He was hoeing out some weeds and smiled as I approached.

'Ah, Mr Rhea. Such a nice surprise. We seldom get a visit by the police.'

The Reverend Jason Chandler was a curious man, in my view. He had done several jobs before entering the ministry of the Church of England, including being a coastguard and a salesman of women's lingerie, and he lived a life remote from the parishioners. He seldom entered the social life of the area and, as a bachelor, found it difficult to mix with the families whom his church served. In his late forties, he was always pleasant when I met him.

'Mr Chandler,' I began, 'I've an odd event to enquire about,' and I related the story of Mr Bradley's remains being found by the hiker.

'Ah, yes,' he said without hesitation. 'He was in my congregation this morning, Mr Rhea. A congregation of one, I might add. And then he collapsed and died. He was sitting in the first pew, so I laid him out and put a sign up asking for prayers. I do hope he goes to Heaven, Mr Rhea. He was a truly generous man, a keen supporter of our little church at Briggsby.'

'Did you call the doctor?' I asked.

'Well, no. I, well, had reached the most solemn part of the service, preparing for communion, you know, when it happened, I had reached the consecration of bread and wine and could not interrupt that ... so when I got to him, it was clear he was dead. I was a coastguard, you know, very highly trained in first aid, and, well, there was no doubt about it. He was too late to receive communion, you know. He passed away just a few minutes too soon, and I know that would not have pleased him. He did like to receive communion, Mr Rhea. Anyway, calling a doctor would have been a total waste of time, far too late to revive him. Far too late. God works in mysterious ways, Mr Rhea.'

'You can say that again!' I could not help myself uttering that remark. 'So what did you do?'

'After I'd laid him out, you mean?'

'Yes.'

'Well, nothing. I felt I ought to put the sign on him to tell visitors he was dead, rather than asleep. People do fall asleep in church, as I'm sure you know, but I felt I ought to make it quite clear that this was a dead man.'

'Which you did. Then what?'

'Well, I had another service immediately afterwards, at Crampton, and had to leave straight away, otherwise I would have kept that congregation waiting – Lord and Lady Crampton always attend on Thursdays, you see.'

'It's a few minutes' drive to Crampton, eh?'

'Yes,' he oozed. 'There is not a moment to spare on that trip, and I had to be on time ... I knew Mrs Dodson would see to Mr Bradley. She does his cottage, you know. She's the church cleaner, as well, so I knew he was in good hands. It's her day in, you see, and I knew she would find him. She was due to do the brasses today and, well, I felt she could not help noticing him.'

'She didn't go in this morning.' I sighed, wondering how on earth people could behave like this, and added for good measure, 'The head fell off her brush.'

'Oh, dear, I do hope she gets it fixed. That church floor does get very dusty, from the road, you know, passing traffic ...'

I had found the last person to see poor old Mr Bradley when he was alive, and I had an account of his final moments, such as they were. After taking a formal statement from the Reverend Mr Chandler, I left him to his gardening and wondered how he would have coped as a coastguard if a ship was about to be grounded. Maybe he would have left it for a fisherman to sort out – which might explain why he was no longer a coastguard.

The post-mortem examination showed that Mr Bradley had died from natural causes, from a heart attack, in fact. There would be no inquest.

We did find his relatives, and they took the body home for burial. I did not tell them of the odd circumstances of the discovery of his body, merely saying he had died in church while attending a service.

That knowledge seemed to offer them some consolation, so I did not say that he had missed Holy Communion.

Sad though sudden death is, there are times when coping with corpses is akin to a black comedy.

Three large policemen, one of whom was myself, once had the tricky job of manoeuvring the corpse of an eighteen-stone man down a narrow, winding staircase while the grieving family sat in a room at the foot of the stairs. The problem was that the corpse had only one leg, so there was precious little to grip as we took it away for a post-mortem. The truth was the fellow got away from us on those stairs and bumped his way down the flight until he ended in a heap on the front door mat. Fortunately the door into the room was closed, and so the relatives never saw what happened; it was also fortunate that the front door was closed, otherwise the one-legged body would have rolled into the street and directly into a bus queue standing outside. The result might have been something like a game of giant skittles.

We had a similar task when a huge woman collapsed on the top of a lighthouse; we had to slide her down the winding staircase because it was impossible to lift her and impossible to manoeuvre the coffin-sized shell around the tight corners. We made use of a card table top and sat her upright on that, then used it as a kind of sledge with her on board. I'm sure the trip gave her a posthumous thrill – it frightened the life out of us, for we felt sure the contraption would escape from our hands on the descent. But it didn't.

I had to admire the improvisation skills of a colleague at Strensford, when he came across a dead man at the back of a pub one Saturday lunchtime. A regular at the pub had found the corpse and thought it was merely a drunk sleeping off his over-indulgence. Because this route led in from the car park, however, and because it was also a busy alley leading to several shops, my colleague had to think fast. He was alone, the local police van was in use at Thirsk Races, and the shell was being utilised at another sudden death. He did not like to leave his body lying on a busy thoroughfare with women and children passing by every few seconds, so he borrowed a wheelbarrow from the landlord, sat the still-warm corpse in it and placed one or two beer bottles around it. Thus the corpse had all the appearance of a drunk, and my colleague wheeled it through the town to the mortuary. He was cheered on his way by some other cheerful drinkers, but no one knew he was carting away a corpse. They thought it was a drunk being arrested in a highly unusual but very practical manner.

Perhaps the funniest that I was involved in, from a slapstick point of view, involved a body in the upper harbour at Strensford.

The call came at seven o'clock one morning, when I was patrolling in uniform, and I was despatched to the power station whose night-duty man had noticed the body with the arrival of dawn. It lay in the mud, apparently having been left high and dry when the tide had receded, and it was that of an elderly man. I went into the control room to ask where precisely this body lay and was shown from an upper window.

'You'll need wellies,' I was told. 'It's thick mud out there.'

I borrowed a pair from the power station's staff room, went down a gangway normally used by boats and started to walk across the expanse of thick black mud. I sank almost to wellington boot tops in the slime, but beneath the layer of greasy mud there was a firm surface, so I decided to continue. The body lay at least fifty yards away, and beyond it the river flowed towards the sea in a channel it had created over the years. When the tide was in, this area of mud flats would be covered with several feet of sea water, but there were some hours before this would happen.

Then, as I lifted my foot to make the next step, the wellington remained in the mud. The depth and the suction held it down, and so I had to walk across to the corpse by literally lifting each wellington up by hand as I walked. Step by step, already filthy around the legs and hands, I made my way to that body. It seemed to take an age, but I arrived to find an old man lying face down in the mud.

The clothes on his back were dry, an indication that he had fallen face down into the waters of the upper harbour. As the tide had flowed out, he had been left marooned on this mud bank. He was dead; of that, I was never in doubt, but I tried to lift the body to examine his face and to make a cursory check for any signs of life.

As I took the weight with my hands, my feet slithered backwards in that slime, and I fell flat on my own face beside the body, sending a shower of black, oily mud towards the skies. I was spreadeagled there and could feel myself sinking, but I managed to draw my legs beneath me to stand upright. I emerged like a black and greasy excrescence and wondered if the power station staff were observing this performance. Once on my feet, now oozing all over with stinking mud, I tried again. But the body would not shift; the suction of the ghastly brew held it firmly down. I splodged around in that smelly scum, trying and trying to slide or lift the body, but in that thick, oily mess it would not move. I stank like a drain now and was smothered because of frequent slips and falls.

I decided I needed help and that bare feet might be one solution, so I trudged back to the power station, leaving my wellies standing on the corpse's rump. They would act as markers for my next sortie. From an outbuilding at the power station, where my condition could not do a lot of harm, I rang for assistance.

The power station staff, now increasing in numbers as the day's work began, laughed themselves sick when they saw me, but I did manage to persuade the sergeant that I needed help. He said he would send someone to help me, and this would be a constable who lived nearby. He was summoned to my aid. When Alan arrived, he fell about laughing at me, and then we set off together across the mud, heading for the pair of wellies which were our guides. The stench from the path I had created by disturbing the mud was appalling. It was like splodging through a huge open-air sewer.

Alan had taken off his shoes and had rolled his trousers up to his knees before accompanying me, but even the act of walking made us slither and catch one another; by the time Alan arrived with me, we were both smothered in stinking black slime. We decided that the only way to turn the body over was for me to stand at one side, grip his clothing and roll him towards me, while Alan stood at the other to lift and push simultaneously. We tried. The body refused to move. Then, as we heaved and pulled, there was, without any warning, a loud sucking sound as the body suddenly moved – I fell backwards into the knee-deep mud, the body came halfway out and Alan fell flat on his face as his feet slithered away. When I stood up, the corpse was on its side with one hand sticking into the air like a mast, and Alan was crawling out of the mire with his entire face and upper body dripping with ooze. But we had dislodged the body from its anchorage.

We managed to get the unfortunate chap out of the sludge and onto his feet and, satisfied that he was really very dead, began to carry him back to the shore. I put one of the dead arms about my shoulders, and Alan did likewise; thus the three of us slithered, fell and stank our way back to the slipway, by which time a cheering crowd had assembled at the power station railings.

Once ashore, we could cope. There had to be a post-mortem on this body, and the odd thing was that he had not died from drowning – there was no water in his lungs. He had died from natural causes. How he came to be in the water was never discovered.

Afterwards I submitted a request for my uniform to be cleaned at the expense of the police, and I was told that no funds were available for that kind of thing. Keeping my uniform pressed and clean for duty was my responsibility, I was told.

But from that day forward, there was always a welcome for me at the power station, with a cup of coffee and the offer of a pair of clean wellies any time I need them to go paddling.

Chapter 7

I hope I shall never be deterred from detecting what I
think is a cheat.

SAMUEL JOHNSON (1709-84)

ONE OF THE CRIMES which puzzled, and probably still
puzzles, the general public was that of taking and driving
away a motor vehicle without having either the consent
of the owner or other lawful authority. This bafflement
has arisen because this is not the same crime as stealing
a motor vehicle. The two are quite distinct, and the
essential difference is that stealing entails the intention
of permanently depriving the owner of his property,
while the unauthorised borrower has no such intention.
He takes a vehicle for a joy-ride, and youths would take
cars simply to get them home after a night out, after
which they would abandon them with little thought of
the owners' anguish or little anxiety about the damage
and expense they had caused the unfortunate owner.
Almost without exception, the cars were found by the
police and restored to their owners.

For some years, this unlawful taking of motor
vehicles was not a crime, simply because it had not been
considered when the early definitions of larceny were
compiled. To prosecute the 'takers' for something, they
were occasionally charged with stealing the petrol they
had consumed. This smacked of desperation, but what
else could be done by the police?

Later, because an increasing number of cars were being 'borrowed' illicitly, the offence was written into the law, albeit not as part of the law on stealing but as part of the 1930's road traffic law. It was another thirty years or so before the law realised that other forms of conveyance were also borrowed without lawful authority and that no statute catered for them. They included bikes, hang-gliders, aircraft, boats, trains and roller-skates – in fact, it now includes anything constructed or adapted for the carriage of persons by land, water or air, whether or not such a thing has an engine fitted. However, it does not include things which are pedestrian-controlled, such as prams and lawnmowers. This long-overdue 1968 law did, of course, continue to include cars, lorries, buses and other such means of transport.

The unlawful borrowing of that mass of other conveyances was not written into the Theft Act until 1968, and so, when I was a young constable and an Aide to CID, I was not concerned with the unauthorised taking of all conveyances but merely with those which fell into the definition of motor vehicles. But we were heavily into the popular crime of Taking Without Consent, as we called it in long-hand, or TWOC as we abbreviated it. We pronounced it TWOCK.

There was no crime of TWOCing a pedal cycle, however (there is now), and so lots of illicit bike-borrowers were never prosecuted simply because they had committed no criminal offence. Now, a bike is within the meaning of a conveyance, and so illegal borrowers can be prosecuted.

One of the more popular crimes when I was an Aide to CID was the relay TWOC. A man would take a car from, say, London and drive it as far as the tank full of petrol permitted – say, Luton. At Luton he would abandon the first car and take another one, driving that until its tank was almost empty. That might have carried him to, say, Newark, where he would seek another one with the keys in the ignition. The Newark car would perhaps be driven to York and left in a side street as he took yet another to convey him to Middlesbrough or further north. And so the journey continued. In this way, a TWOC merchant could travel the length or breadth of Britain without cost to himself, but leaving in his wake a trail of abandoned motor vehicles.

The sufferers were the owners of the cars. Sometimes the cars were damaged; sometimes they were abandoned in awkward places as their tanks ran dry, and sometimes they were never found at all. If they were found abandoned, it rested upon the unfortunate owner to recover them, and so their owners had to travel long distances at their own expense to fetch home their straying vehicles. Sometimes, as a matter of courtesy and as a means of further protecting these abandoned cars, we would take them to the police station for security.

One such case of relay TWOC occurred while I was doing my stint as an Aide at Eltering.

The message originated from the Metropolitan Police in London and it said that a car taken from Putney had been found abandoned at St Albans; one taken at St Albans had been found abandoned at Peterborough; one taken at Peterborough had been found abandoned at Doncaster, and one had been stolen at Doncaster only that afternoon. That had not yet been found, and so all police forces within reach of the A1 (the Great North Road) were being alerted. It seemed that a relay TWOC merchant was driving north via the A1, venturing off only to abandon one car and take another.

The car stolen from Doncaster was a black Humber Snipe, and its registration number was HMH 200. We were requested to seek this car in our area, where it might have been abandoned. We are also advised to alert our officers to the likelihood of a theft or TWOC in our part of the country.

At half-past seven that same evening, one of the uniformed constables of Eltering rang in from a telephone kiosk to say he had found the abandoned Humber Snipe. There was no one with the car, the keys were still in the ignition, and it was presently on a piece of waste ground in the town. He was told not to touch it until the CID arrived. Detective Sergeant Connolly was told of the car and said to me, 'Go and have a look at it, Nick. There's not a lot we can do with a job of this kind, but see if there's any stolen property stashed away in it, fingerprints on the fascia, that sort of thing.'

I joined PC Steve Forman at the car. He had found it during a routine foot patrol and watched as I opened the boot, lifted the seats and did a thorough search without finding anything of interest. With a light fingerprint brush laced with grey powder, I dusted the steering-wheel, internal mirror, ashtray and other points likely to have been handled by the driver, but none was worth preserving. They were all smudged.

I made an external examination of the car. I noted that it bore the number plates MHH 200, which had not been altered or replaced by false ones, and saw that it was in a filthy condition. Its general appearance was one of neglect but it did bear a current Road Fund Licence, as the excise licence was then known. This was before the days of MOT tests, and the tyres were bald, the interior was full of dust and corn husks, old sacks and rusting tools, and there were holes under the mudguards and in the doors.

'Is there any petrol in it?' I asked Steve.

He switched on the ignition, and the gauge showed empty, although by shaking the car with the filler cap off, we could hear a faint sloshing in the tank.

'He's run it dry,' I said. 'But I reckon there's enough to get it back to the station. I'll drive it there for safe keeping.'

And so we both jumped in and I drove it to Eltering Police Station, where I parked in the compound at the rear, locked it and brought the keys into the office.

Steve and I made out our reports and settled down to await the inevitable report of a car missing from Eltering. If the Humber had been abandoned here, another one would have been stolen – unless, of course, the TWOC merchant was travelling no further than Eltering. In that case, he could be at home now, gloating over his triumph of travelling free from London. But we felt this was not the case. We felt sure we were part of a relay series of TWOCs and that soon a worried car-owner would turn up to report his or her car missing.

Sure enough, a couple of hours later, as I was typing some statements in the general office, a man arrived on a bike and came to the enquiry desk. He was dressed in rough working clothes and smelt of pigs.

'Noo then,' he said as he came in, wafting that awful pig muck aroma around as he removed his flat cap, 'Ah think this is t'right spot to come, but somebody's pinched my car.'

'This is the right spot.' PC John Rogers tried to hold his nose away from the pervading pong, but there was no escape. 'So, let's start at the beginning.'

The man was called Ralph Cross. He was a farm

labourer and he lived in Eltering. After taking those details on the form he was compiling, Rogers asked, 'Now, Mr Cross, the car. What kind is it?'

'Humber Snipe,' he said. 'A black 'un. Mucky, mind, but black underneath all t' muck. Number MHH 200. They've took it from that spare land up Penthorne Lane way. They won't get far in her because she's hardly gitten any petrol in. Anyroad, Ah thowt Ah'd tell you fellers.'

Upon hearing his description, I came to the counter. 'Mr Cross,' I asked, 'where was it taken from? You've not been in Doncaster today, have you?'

'Doncaster?' he sounded horrified. 'Nay, lad, not Doncaster. That's down south, isn't it?'

'It's a long way south of here, yes,' I agreed. 'But we got a report to say your car had been stolen from Doncaster.'

I turned up the relevant message in the Occurrence Book and read it again.

'Nay, there's summat wrang there,' he frowned. 'She's nobbut been to Scarborough once and that was six month back, and she's nivver been as far south as Doncaster, nivver.'

It now began to look as if a highly improbable thing had happened. I wondered if someone had stolen Cross's Humber Snipe from Eltering that morning and had then driven it to Doncaster, there to abandon it without this man's ever realizing it had gone missing. And had someone else then stolen it again, and driven it back to its home town, a sheer fluke of circumstance, but not impossible. But no – that was not possible, because who had reported it missing from Doncaster?

If Cross had not known it was missing, he could not have reported it ... unless the car had been involved in some other adventure we knew nothing about ...

We had a puzzle, and I wondered whether there was some insurance fiddle going on or whether Cross was involved in some other kind of wrong-doing of a very subtle kind. Should we tell him straightaway that his car had been found and that it had been abandoned here in town after being reported missing at Doncaster? Or should we find out exactly what had occurred before releasing it? We continued with our enquiries.

'I'll ring Doncaster police,' said John Rogers, and he said to Cross, 'We had a report of your car being in Doncaster this morning,' avoiding mention of the reported theft in that town.

'It nivver was!' he cried. 'I went up to t'farm in it this morning, drove a few sacks o' taties about, and a piglet to t'vets, and then it was in t'farmyard till I left at half five tonight. She's nivver been in Doncaster today, no, nivver.'

Rogers knew he must check this tale with Doncaster, even before circulating Mr Cross's car as stolen or TWOC'd. Cross and I watched as he put through his call.

'Ah,' he said eventually as the call was connected. 'This is PC Rogers from Eltering. I'm ringing about that Humber Snipe, the black one ...'

We could not hear any response but were to learn that the officer said, 'Forget it, Mr Rogers. It's been found abandoned in Wakefield. The owner's gone to collect it.'

'You're joking!' he cried.

'No, it's been recovered. The black Humber Snipe that we circulated as a relay runner, HMH 200.'

'But we have it here, in Eltering ...'

'No, you haven't. Wakefield police have it, and it's safe and sound in their compound, awaiting collection. It was found abandoned there at five o'clock this evening.'

'Well, if you are sure ...'

'We are,' said Doncaster, and Rogers put down his telephone, puzzlement showing on his face.

'They've found it in Wakefield ...'

'Wakefield?' cried Cross. 'Does that mean I've got to go to Wakefield to get it back?'

'Five o'clock it was found, they said,' continued Rogers. 'And the owner is already on his way to collect it.'

'Now, hang on a minute, lads, at five o'clock Ah was in my car, driving home, and Ah was here in Eltering, nowhere near Doncaster or Wakefield or any o' them spots.'

In the meantime, I had picked up the occurrence book and was looking at the entry relating to the Doncaster Humber.

And then, embarrassed until my face flushed deep crimson, I said to Mr Cross, 'Mr Cross, your car has been recovered, but it is not at Wakefield. It is here, in our compound.'

'What the hell's going on then?' He looked at us one by one.

'We thought a black Humber Snipe, stolen at Doncaster had been abandoned here. It's HMH 200.'

'That's not mine,' he said rapidly. 'Mine's MHH 200. Different number, different car.'

And so it was.

Highly embarrassed, we returned his car to him and did our best to explain, but he drove off cheerfully, saying, 'I'm glad you fellers found mine.'

'All part of our duty, Mr Cross.' I said.

And then I asked John Rogers, 'Where did he park his car after work?'

'Outside his house,' he said. 'On waste land at Penthorne Lane.'

'That isn't where we found it,' I said. 'We looked at it on waste land just off the Sycamore estate. That's on the other side of the town.'

I looked at John Rogers and he looked at me. 'So it had been nicked after all,' he said.

'And found abandoned, and returned to the owner,' I said.

'So the file is closed?' grinned John.

'Yes,' I said, with more than a hint of relief. 'One crime reported and one crime detected, with all the property recovered intact. A nice entry for our records.'

'And a piece of fine detective work,' laughed John. 'You know, we were idiots not to have noticed those car numbers were different.'

'Round numbers are always false,' I said quoting from Samuel Johnson because I could think of nothing else worth saying.

One of the most peculiar TWOC cases concerned a bus, and we never did find the perpetrator of this cheeky crime.

A Women's Institute from County Durham had hired a coach from Palatine Pullman, a local coach-hire company, to take a party of ladies on a pleasure outing to the North York Moors. One of their halts was at Eltering, where they were to be given a guided tour of Eltering Castle, known for its links with the Plantagenets, and afterwards they would have lunch at the White Hart Inn. Their total stay in the town was scheduled to take 1¾ hours; they arrived at noon and were to leave at 1.45 p.m.

The splendid coach parked in Castle Drive to disgorge its ladies, and the driver did as most drivers do

– he ate his own sandwiches and drank his flask of coffee while sitting on the luxurious back seat, and then curled up on the long, relaxing seat and went to sleep. It was something he did regularly on such trips. He left the passenger entrance door unlocked, because he knew the noise and chatter of the returning ladies would rouse him. It always did. His own little cab was also unlocked – and he left the keys in the ignition; again, he always did this because there had never been any bother.

What happened next is something of a mystery, but, in reconstructing the events, it seems that a cheeky character had seen what he thought was an empty coach and had climbed aboard, seen the keys in the ignition and then driven the bus over the moors to Strensford.

News of the disappearance of the bus came from the WI's organiser who had travelled with the party. She came to the police station at Eltering, harassed and red-faced.

'Our driver's gone without us,' she panted. 'We were not late, there has been no delay, and he has left the place where we parked.'

This kind of problem occurred a lot in popular tourist areas, and invariably the panic was due to a misunderstanding of some kind. Either the ladies had not understood where the bus would be upon departure or they'd taken the wrong turning on the way back to it, or it would be in the coach park in town. Invariably, in such cases, we managed to reunite bus and passengers.

So, well-practised in this art and with the aid of the town's uniform branch, we searched every likely parking place, but there was no sign of the distinctive coach.

PC John Rogers, who knew every inch of the town realised the lady was right – her coach had gone and so had the driver.

'I'll ring the owners,' he offered.

He rang them and said, 'Oh, this is Eltering Police. I'm ringing on behalf of a WI outing; they've come here on one of your coaches. Yes, today.'

He waited as the receptionist plugged him through to someone else, and then he repeated his story, adding, 'Well, there is now a problem. The bus has gone, but its passengers are still here. We have about forty-five ladies marooned in Eltering. All wanting to catch their bus to its next destination. But there is no bus. We have searched the town, and there is no sign of it. And they were not late, not lost, not rude to the driver or anything like that. The bus has not been dismissed and it has not caught fire anywhere. Now, has the driver called you at all? Is there any explanation from him? No, he's not reported it missing because he's missing as well.'

From what we could overhear, it seemed the driver had not been in touch with his head office, and they could offer no explanation. It was now 2.15 p.m. and the ladies were getting anxious, either wishing to travel onwards or, in some cases, wanting to get back home. With the co-operation of the WI organiser and the coach company, John Rogers managed to persuade them to wait for an hour. His calm, unflappable response had a soothing effect upon the WI organiser.

'Things might sort themselves out,' he said, raising his eyes to Heaven. 'I'm sure the driver has not forgotten you.'

The company agreed to this compromise, threatening to discipline their driver if and when he turned up, and they agreed that, if he did not return to the pre-arranged place by 3.15 p.m., they would dispatch a duplicate coach. But it would take an hour and a half to reach Eltering. The ladies were heading for a lot of tea-drinking, some delightful window shopping and a fair bit of queueing at loos. The organiser said she would go and explain things to her clients, then return at 3.15 p.m. to see if there was any further development.

When she'd gone, I smiled at John Rogers. 'What do you make of all that?' I asked.

'He'll have gone off to the loo himself, or for a meal somewhere. Mebbe got a puncture on the way back … He'll turn up. They always do.' He was philosophical about it. 'We get loads of problems like that.'

As the bus had not been reported stolen and as the driver was evidently still with it, we did not circulate it as a stolen vehicle, nor did we think it had been taken without consent. In fact, that is what had happened. A man had driven it across the moors to Strensford, and all the time the driver remained asleep on that rear seat, blissfully unaware of his predicament. The warmth and the gentle motion lulled him, and so, as the bus motored its expensive way across the heights towards the coast, the driver went into an even deeper sleep.

Having arrived safely at his destination in Strensford, the thief (or, to be precise, the Taker-Without-Consent) simply drove the bus into a quiet street, parked it and walked away. There is every reason for believing he had no idea he had taken the driver with him.

The driver, a man called Jimmy Porritt, was aroused by the cessation of the relaxing motion. A few moments after the bus had stopped and its temporary driver departed, he yawned, stretched his arms and awoke from a very pleasant dream. He left his place and walked down the aisle to his driving seat, never at this stage thinking he was in the wrong town. He settled down and then looked at his watch. It was 3 p.m.

Puzzled that his ladies had not returned on time, he

looked outside and then saw he was in an unfamiliar street ... and there was no sign of Eltering Castle. Jimmy was baffled. He felt sure he'd parked near Eltering Castle and yet, in this place, he could hear seagulls screaming, and between the houses he could see the tall shape of a lighthouse.

He clambered out of his bus, puzzled and somewhat alarmed, thinking perhaps that he had lost his senses or had a blackout of some kind. He hailed a passing lady with a baby in a pram and said, 'Excuse me, but what street is this?'

'Albion Terrace,' she said.

'Ah.' He did not wish to appear foolish, but had to ask, 'And what town is it?'

'Strensford,' she said, puzzled by his question.

He returned to his coach utterly confused by this turn of events, and in his bewilderment decided to ask the police to enlighten him. The police at Strensford listened to his odd tale and decided to seek our help in sorting out this Jimmy's dilemma.

John Rogers took the call, and I heard him chuckling. 'Yes,' I heard him say. 'We have lost a bus; it's left a load of women in town. They're overcrowding all the loos after drinking gallons of tea till we got things sorted out.'

'I'll get him to come back to Eltering,' said the Strensford constable. 'Shall I ask him to park near the castle where he was before?'

'Yes, do that,' John agreed.

When the WI organiser returned, within a few minutes of this call, we could say that her bus had been found in Strensford, but we had no idea why it had gone there. The driver was full of apologies and he would return within the hour. We also rang his head office to say the ladies and their coach had been re-united, but we left any explanations to the driver.

We never did receive a formal complaint that this coach had been the subject of a 'take and drive away' offence, but I did wonder if there was an offence of taking a driver without consent!

One vehicle which caused some legal head-scratching was the caravan.

If people lived in it, either temporarily or permanently, was it a dwelling-house? Or, if it was used only for holidays, was it a storehouse when not in use, for it then contained only furniture and crockery? Were those caravans used as temporary offices classified as offices, or was a caravan merely a trailer, as defined in the various road traffic regulations? One caravan at Aidensfield had an onion-shaped edifice on its roof and was used for Greek Orthodox Church services, so was that particular caravan a church? If so, it would be sacrilege to break into it, or burglary when such a vehicle was used as living accommodation.

We would pose questions such as: if someone stole a residential caravan, did they steal an entire dwelling-house? But stealing a dwelling-house was legally impossible, because it was attached to the realty, i.e. the ground. To be legally guilty of stealing a real dwelling-house, it was necessary for the house to be demolished and abandoned, and then someone who stole the stones might be found guilty. So, for theft purposes, we felt a caravan should be regarded as merely a trailer. Was it a just thing to change the nomenclature of a caravan in order to accommodate particular laws? And what about the contents? If a stolen caravan contained 250 different items of furniture, crockery and food, was the thief guilty of stealing all those as well as the caravan itself?

These little puzzles were cast into the pool during our initial training, just to alert us to the legal fiction which was then so much a part of criminal law, and to attune our minds, through argument and illustration, to the wiles of both lawyers and villains in their desire to find ways around the various rules and regulations. It was interesting to realise that lawyers could spend lots of hours poring over lots of books to solve this kind of problem while earning lots of cash, but we poor constables had to carry the information in our heads. Instead of taking days or weeks to arrive at a decision, we had to act promptly and fairly in our execution of the law, without bringing the wrath of public opinion down upon our heads.

Although some of the answers to these knotty issues could be found in statutory form, others never received a satisfactory answer. But our discussions did cause some mirth and some interest while we were learning the law.

One thing we did know, however, was that a caravan could not be the subject of a TWOC charge. As TWOC then applied only to motor vehicles, there was a legal puzzle if someone took without consent a car with a caravan attached. The car could be TWOC'd, but the trailer could not. In its case, it was either theft or nothing.

However, at Eltering we were presented with another puzzle associated with a caravan.

David Crossley was a self-employed builder in his middle thirties who undertook odd jobs in and around Eltering. He could build a fine stone house if requested but seemed to spend most of his time repairing old buildings, roofing farms and cottages, constructing walls and renovating a wide range of rural edifices, from pigsties to church steeples. He was a competent workman, and we never had complaints about either his craftsmanship or his honesty. He would never be rich – he lacked the entrepreneurial skills necessary to be a tycoon, but he did earn a reasonable living for himself, his wife and two sons.

To put this story into chronological order, David was commissioned to build a row of stables for a local farmer who fancied himself as a member of the landed gentry. The farmer, Andrew Farrell, had become wealthy by the easiest possible route – he had married a rich wife. Her links with the gentry of the county and with local aristocrats meant that Andrew had to keep up appearances.

After a year or two of bliss, which included Andrew's obligatory attendance at hunt balls in country houses, fox-hunting with the nobility and shooting with golden retrievers called Rufus and Polly, it became evident that his wife was no fool. The blessed honeymoon over, Andrew found himself actually having to work to maintain the life-style to which he wanted to become accustomed.

But if he had acquired almost the right accent, almost the right clothes sense, almost the right way of holding wine glasses, and the ability to say 'grarse' instead of 'grass' and 'bass' instead of 'bus', he did lack the ability to make enough money to win over the friends he so desperately wished to cultivate.

Keeping horses for hunting, eventing and even racing was one of his ideas; horses, he knew, did open lots of doors to a finer style of living, and although his wife, Angela, spent a lot of money on herself in the way of clothes, outings and smart cars, she made Andrew work for his place in her society. Those of us on the outside of this domestic drama knew that Andrew would never achieve his social goals, but Andrew did not cease to strive in his efforts.

And so it was that David Crossley found himself building a block of eight stables in the grounds of the Farrell house, once called Honeywell Farm but now known as Honeywell Hall, in keeping with Andrew's new image.

David was sensible enough to get Andrew to pay for the materials and part of the labour costs as the building progressed. But by the time the smart new block was complete and Andrew's fine stables received their first intake of handsome fillies and colts, David had not received his final payment. He was owed some £800 in labour charges, but repeated requests did not produce the cash from Andrew.

We all suspected that Andrew's desire for social acceptance in high places had put a strain on his bank balance, a strain that was affecting other tradesfolk and business people in addition to David Crossley. News of Andrew's impending disaster had filtered through to the CID, not because getting into debt is a criminal offence but because people were openly talking about Andrew's inability to meet his rising social expenses. If his wife did indeed have money of her own, she was not letting her husband get his hands on it.

Then Andrew himself came into the office at Eltering one fine spring morning and was referred to the CID. I took him into our tiny office.

'Well, Mr Farrell,' I said, 'how can we help?'

'Someone's stolen my caravan,' he said, and I could see the theft had deeply upset him. 'It's disappeared sometime since yesterday afternoon.'

I quizzed him about it. He had bought it only a week earlier, second-hand but in excellent condition, from a supplier near York. It was a four-berth model, fully equipped with sleeping and kitchen equipment. It was worth, he felt, about £400 – that's what he'd paid for it.

He'd seen it in position the previous afternoon, at 4.30 p.m., and had missed it at ten o'clock that morning. It stood on a concrete hardstanding adjoining his new stable block, and it was to have accommodated a new groom he had appointed to care for his increasing number of horses.

'It's vital I get it back, Mr Rhea,' he said. 'I need that man to work with my horses, otherwise I shall lose valuable customers … and there is nowhere else for him to sleep. He has no transport, and there's no accommodation available nearby; besides, he needs to be close at hand at all times …'

I obtained a detailed description of the missing caravan but realised there were no distinguishing marks upon it; this was one of the Nomad range, all being very similar to each other. Farrell's caravan did bear his car's registration number but that could easily be removed. However, I assured him details would be circulated and asked him if he could point to any suspects.

I got the impression that he was reluctant to answer that question, but when I said that recovery of the caravan depended upon his total co-operation, he said, 'Yes, well, not just one suspect. Several.'

'Several?' I was surprised and must have sounded it, because he produced a handwritten note from his wallet. It was on lined paper from a cheap writing-pad, and in ballpoint pen were the words, 'When you pay your bill, you'll get your caravan back.'

'What bill is this?' I asked.

He shrugged his shoulders and had a look of defeat about him. 'I don't know, Mr Rhea,' he admitted. 'I'm

135

being honest with you now – I owe lots and lots, to umpteen different tradesmen. The butcher, the garage, the farrier, the chap who delivers food for my cattle and horses, the bank of course ... You see, I can't afford to let this groom go, and he will, if there's no accommodation and no room in the house. Besides, my wife won't have him in the house, being just a groom, you understand ...'

I could see he was in dire trouble, but that was not our concern. I made a list of those to whom he owed money and decided I would interview them all to see if any of them admitted removal of the caravan. One obvious starting point was anyone on his list who had a car or Landrover fitted with a towbar. But when I discreetly inspected the vehicles owned by Farrell's nominees, at least eight of them had towbars ...

It took a few days to trace and interview each of these suspects. I found them all, asked about the money that was owed to them by Farrell and then questioned them about the caravan. None admitted anything. In spite of our circulations, there was no news of its whereabouts, and it seemed it was going to be lost forever, adding one more undetected crime to our statistics.

Then, some five or six weeks afterwards, I got another call which, on the face of it, had nothing to do with this case.

'It's Hull City Police,' said a voice. 'D/C Casson speaking.'

'D/C Rhea at this end,' I replied. 'How can I help?'

'We've had a spate of housebreakings and shopbreakings in and around Hull,' he said. 'We've got a suspect in, a good 'un, I might add, and he's implicated a mate of his. The mate is thought to be in possession of some of the nicked goods, household things. Among the identifiable stuff is a Bush radio – we've got the serial number; he's got away with some tinned foods and crockery, and other odds and ends from houses. Apart from nicking cash, he's also got himself kitted out for his holiday by pinching everything he needs.'

'And you think he's on holiday with his ill-gotten gains on our patch?'

'We're sure he is, him and his girlfriend. He's called Mills, Peter Henry Mills, and his girl is Susan Dunn. We don't think she's implicated, but if you bring her in, she might be able to tell us something useful.'

I took details of the couple, and a description of their physical appearance, and then he said, 'They're holidaying in a caravan. The address we have is Mill Close, Pattington. Is that on your patch?'

'It's in this sub-division,' I confirmed. 'What do you want us to do, precisely?'

'Arrest them both on suspicion of committing our crimes, seal the caravan in case it's full of stolen goods and detain them in your cells till I get there.'

'Right, I'll have words with my D/S, but I can see no problem. Shall we ring to let you know when they're inside?'

'I'd appreciate that.'

Gerry Connolly and I drove to Pattington, which is a pretty village between Ashfordly and York. Brick-built houses line an interesting street, and we had no difficulty finding Mill Close in a small valley behind the church. It was a disused flour mill on the banks of a stream, and the old millwheel was still in working condition. Tucked into a corner of a field behind the mill were half a dozen caravans, most of which appeared to be occupied by visitors. Cars stood beside each one, so I looked for a car bearing a Hull registration plate, i.e. one with a sequence of letters ending in either AT, KH or RH. There had been no mention of a car by the Hull CID, but Mills would need one to reach here – besides, he might have borrowed one, hired one or even bought one, or his girl might have done likewise. This was not a cast-iron method of locating him, for he could have got his car from anywhere, but such checks often produced a good starting point. And in this case, it did. We found a Morris Minor beside a caravan, and it bore the Hull registration letters AKH.

As Gerry and I approached the caravan, I noticed it was a Nomad but at that stage had no reason to connect it with the one missing from Farrell's farm. It was just one of many on this site, and it had been backed into a hedgerow, which meant we did not notice its number plate. And we never thought of looking.

The couple inside, who admitted being Peter Henry Mills and Susan Dunn, offered no resistance, although he protested his innocence at the accusations we levelled at him, and she stood up for him, in her innocence. We took the caravan keys and those of the car, which had been hired for the week, and locked both before we drove the couple to the police station pending the arrival of officers from Hull.

On the way into the office, Gerry was quietly quizzing them.

'Your caravan, is it?' he asked. 'Do you rent the space all the year?'

'It's not mine,' said Mills affably. 'I saw this advert in the *Hull Daily Mail*; I rent it from a chap who lives up here; he's got all those you saw just now. Chap called Crossley, a builder, he is.'

And then the warning bells rang in my head. I began to wonder if that caravan belonged to Andrew Farrell.

Crossley was owed money, he did have a vehicle capable of towing such a caravan away, and here it was, anonymous among lots of others and now being rented out to holidaymakers.

I spoke nothing of my suspicions at this stage, but when we had placed Mills and Dunn in separate cells, having secured the services of a policewoman from Strensford to look after the woman, I voiced my suspicions to Gerry Connolly.

'Seems you'd better have words with our friend Crossley, then,' he beamed.

I found David Crossley at home that evening, and he welcomed me indoors; at my request, we went into the room which served as his office, away from his wife and family.

'David,' I said, 'you might know why I am here.'

'Still chasing Farrell's caravan, are you?' He was pleasant enough.

'I think I've found it,' I said. 'On your little holiday site at Pattington, at the old mill. You let it to a wanted housebreaker from Hull, David. He's just been arrested and the caravan has been sealed off.'

He laughed aloud. 'A fair cop, isn't that what they say? But I haven't stolen it, Mr Rhea. I'm not dishonest. I've just removed it temporarily, hidden it from him, until he pays me what he owes. And when he pays me, he can have it back.'

'A court would say that, as you have been making use of it for personal gain, you had every intention of permanently depriving Farrell of it. That makes it theft.'

'Nobody else has used it, Mr Rhea; that couple from Hull, Mills and Dunn, came without booking – they'd seen my adverts in the paper for the other vans, and came on spec.'

He said they were a one-off let, that he'd had no plans to rent this particular vehicle.

I pondered upon his culpability. If he had a claim of right to that caravan, a claim made in good faith, and if he also had no intention of permanently depriving Farrell of his caravan, there was no crime. But that issue was not for the police to decide – it was for a court of law to determine.

I did not arrest Crossley but told him I would have to report all the facts for consideration by my senior officers. When I told Gerry Connolly, he threw his hands into the air in horror, saying, 'Why does life have to be so bloody complicated? I'll tell Farrell what has happened.'

When Farrell heard the tale, he expressed some relief but no surprise, and then said to Gerry, 'Sergeant, I do not wish to press charges. I will not prosecute David Crossley.'

'You've no choice,' said Connolly. 'A crime has been committed.'

But his desire not to prosecute did sway our chief constable, for he read the file because of its curious nature; he sought the advice of the county solicitor before deciding whether or not to send the papers to the Director of Public Prosecutions for his advice. Because of the odd facts, all the recommendations were for no prosecution.

And so Peter Henry Mills was taken to Hull, along with several identifiable stolen goods from the caravan, and Susan Dunn was released without charge. She said she would stand by him for ever and ever and accused us of planting the stolen radio in the caravan.

And when we examined the caravan more closely, we did find that it still bore the registration number of Andrew Farrell's car. This was evidence in support of

Crossley's claim that he had removed the caravan as a means of retrieving what was owed to him.

It was three weeks later when I bumped into Andrew Farrell in the street.

'Ah, Mr Rhea,' he said. 'Thanks for sorting out that caravan job for me. I think your sergeant was very accommodating in the circumstances, but if I had known it was David Crossley, I'd never have reported it stolen in the first place. I'm letting him keep it as a holiday letting caravan for this season, or until he makes the equivalent of the money I owe him, with a bit extra, of course, for tax.'

'That's good of you.'

'Yes, well, I don't want to bankrupt him, and it's one way of helping me and him. I have found accommodation for my groom – he's in the attic of our house. Angela did agree at length, and so things are working out now. I am making money with the horses too, so I will be able to pay my debts – in time, of course.'

'So all's well that ends well, eh?' I smiled.

'Well, actually, all this might have done me good, given me a superb idea for making more money.'

'Really?' I asked.

'Yes, a caravan site in our fields, for holidaymakers and caravan rallies. A site of static vans and touring vans, a large complex, of course, with toilets and shower facilities, and a farm shop, all to cater for visitors from overseas and even people in permanent residence ... I think that is my next project, Mr Rhea, subject to planning permission, of course.'

I wished him every success but did wonder what Angela would think of masses of tourists and caravans defacing the views from her magnificent home.

I rather felt Andrew would have another fight ahead, but he was a trier. And for that, he deserved credit.

Chapter 8

Riddle of destiny, who can show
What thy short visit meant?
CHARLES LAMB (1775-1834)

SNEAK THIEVES ARE AMONG the most loathsome of creatures. Through their personal greed and odious behaviour, they not only deprive people of their valuables but also cast a dark and depressing cloud of suspicion over many innocent people. In some cases, where the thief is not identified and caught, that suspicion can endure for a long, long time. For this reason alone, a sneak thief is one of the most repulsive of criminals. Sometimes, I think the word 'sneak' is an anagram of snake, snakes being the most lowly and despised of creatures, while 'a snake in the grass' is the term applied to a hidden enemy and a disguised danger. Those feelings may well apply to the sneak thieves who operate in any establishment.

It is a sad fact that these vermin are found in many places where numbers of people congregate. They frequent dance halls, sports centres, swimming pools, offices, factories and other places of work, private parties and even social gatherings of all sizes. Much of their evil trade never reaches the official ears of the police service because the organization which harbours them prefers not to create even more alarm by encouraging an investigation. The result is that many sneak-thieves, having created an atmosphere of distrust, continue to operate.

The police see an arrest as highly beneficial to all honest citizens and a release by many from suspicion. That is one of the real strengths of true liberty, the feeling of being free within the law. There is no civil liberty when innocent people remain under suspicion of being thieves while the real thief, for whatever reason, is allowed to continue his or her nefarious activities.

Thefts by sneak thieves range from the goods which they help to manufacture via the office supplies which help to keep the business in operation to cash and valuables taken from coats and bags left in cloakrooms. Some regard their thieving as a perk of the job and justify it accordingly, especially if they are on low wages, but police records are full of the names of people caught stealing from their place of work. This is theft, and today it carries a maximum penalty of ten years' imprisonment, even if the thief only gets away with a piece of cheese, a brick or the contents of a charity collecting box. Clearly, sentences of that magnitude are not given for minor transgressions, but it remains the case that ten years is the maximum possible sentence for stealing.

It is a sad fact that some people cannot help stealing. There are kleptomaniacs everywhere – they steal cups and saucers from cafés, towels from hotels, spoons from British Railways, cash from their friends or families, food from the canteen or jars of coffee from the stockroom. They will pinch anything and seem not to care that their activities are crimes or that they place others under suspicion and, in some cases, put the jobs and livelihood of their colleagues at risk by pilfering from their employers' profits.

It follows that, where the police are notified that a sneak thief is active, they make very serious attempts to arrest or at least deter the perpetrator. Happily, there are many scientific aids and modern technological methods which are capable of trapping persistent sneak thieves.

One aspect of their crimes is that they are usually repeated, not only once but time and time again. A thief who has successfully purloined a side of bacon from the firm's canteen or stolen cash from the till will try to take more, then more, and yet still more … and in this way they generally trap themselves, with a little help from the police.

I found myself investigating this type of crime soon after I began my attachment to Eltering CID, and it involved the hall which adjoined the Anglican church of St Erasmus. The hall was a busy one and was in use most days of the week, with regular events such as hunt balls, dances, whist drives, evening classes and afternoon classes, craft fairs, private parties and a range of other popular events. It had even hosted a dog show, a model railway exhibition and a ballet dancing display. It was a fine, spacious building with a superb sprung dance floor of polished wood, a balcony for observers, an ante-room for use as a bar, and two large cloakrooms standing at either side of the impressive entrance hall.

The chairman of the St Erasmus Hall Social Committee was Mr Aaron Eyles, a retired butcher, and he called at the police station one Monday morning.

'Ah've a bit of a delicate matter to discuss,' was his opening remark, 'summat that'll not do with being spread around.'

The station duty constable knew old Aaron very well and managed to elicit the fact that he wished to discuss some crimes at the church hall, crimes of a highly sensitive nature, and so John referred him to the CID. Gerry Connolly invited him into his office and offered him a chair and a cup of coffee. I took in the two coffees, and Gerry said, 'Sit down, Nick. Fetch your coffee in here,' then introduced us. He made it clear to Aaron that I was utterly reliable and would not spread gossip about the town.

'So, Aaron, these crimes,' said Gerry. 'What are they?'

'Sneak thieves, Mr Connolly. Somebody's pinching from t'ladies' cloakrooms at St Erasmus's. Bit o' cash, cosmetics, purses, umbrellas even. Daft things like that – one woman's lost a torch, and somebody else has had a new scarf pinched.'

'Over what sort of period, Aaron?' asked Connolly.

'Six months mebbe. Mebbe a bit longer.'

'And you've not reported any to us, is that right? I can't recall any reports.'

'Nay, we haven't. T'committee thought they could fettle it themselves. Ah think some of them thought them thefts were not really thefts, tha knaws; they thought it was folks forgetting where they'd putten things, you know what folks are.'

'I know what folks are,' agreed Connolly. 'So, when are the things vanishing? I thought you had cloakroom attendants at all your dos.'

'Nearly all, Mr Connolly. Some of t'private hirings don't use attendants; Ah mean, a wedding wouldn't bother with 'em, and they sometimes don't get asked for t'smaller jobs. It costs, you see; they get paid by the hour, and t'hirer has to pay.'

'And are all the things vanishing from the ladies' cloakroom?'

He nodded and there was sadness in his eyes. 'Aye,'

he said softly. 'That's t'problem. You see, Ada Clarkson is attendant in the ladies' end. Now she's been doing that job for years, Mr Connolly, with never a hint of owt going wrong. Never a hint. Ah mean, she's churchwarden, she cleans t'church and organises flower rotas, she's into charitable work in town, helps old folks, the blind, the infirm … you couldn't find a more helpful, honest woman.'

'And the stuff is going when Ada is on duty?' I could see Connolly hated to disillusion this old man but he was merely echoing the thoughts that poor old Aaron was entertaining.

'Aye,' he said. 'That's true. At first, folks were reporting the thefts to Ada but they stopped when nowt was done. So they come to me or t'secretary now – that's young Miss McCowey, Alec's lass.'

'And have you mentioned anything to Ada?' asked Gerry.

'Not for t'last month, Mr Connolly. Ah thowt Ah'd give her t'benefit of my doubts, in a manner of speaking, but Ah kept a record of complaints. There's been four late dances, two evening classes and a demonstration of cooking by gas in the evening, and in all cases Ada was working. During each of the four dances, money went from t'ladies' cloakroom, Mr Connolly, and Ah don't know what to make of it.'

Connolly was firm with him. 'Aaron, some of the most unlikely people turn to crime for all kinds of reasons. Ada is mebbe going through a crisis … is she passing through the menopause, eh? Doing things not in character? That's if it is her. We might be making too many accusations without doing the necessary investigations. We might be making assumptions that are wrong.'

'Aye, well, Ah've been through it time and time again, trying to tell myself it can't be Ada, never in a million years, but it all points to her, Mr Connolly. Ah daren't face her about it ...'

'Someone will have to, Aaron.'

'Aye, Ah know. But Ah couldn't. Ah just couldn't. Ah'll be honest with you. Ah couldn't face her, not Ada, not after all t'happy times we've had and the wonderful work she's done for t'church and t'people of Eltering. Ah mean, you couldn't find a better woman, a more honest worker.'

'But in spite of that, you sound convinced of her guilt? If she's as honest as you say, it could be somebody else. What about her companion, the man who operates the gents' cloakroom?'

'Harry Nattrass? Honest as the day is long, he is, an' all. There's nowt gone from his cloakroom, Mr Connolly, not ever.'

'And he's a church worker as well, is he?'

'Not particularly. He does this job as an interest, really. He's got a full-time job. He works in a grocer's shop in town, Major's. Not much of a job, but he's content.'

'Ages? How old are they?'

Connolly was thinking of Ada's possible menopause, for we knew that some women who were going through that difficult phase of their lives were prone to shoplifting.

'Ada? She'll be fiftyish. She's got a grown-up family, both married. Husband's a churchwarden an' all. He works for Langton's Garage, a mechanic.'

'And Harry?'

'Forty mebbe. Married with two bairns, having a struggle to live on his wage – shop assistants aren't well paid, Mr Connolly, and Ah happen to know he's having to take care what he spends. He never has new clothes, can't afford to run a car and hardly ever goes for a drink, so he takes part-time jobs to make ends meet.'

'A suitable candidate for our suspicious minds, eh?' said Connolly. 'He can't make ends meet, his growing family need clothes, shoes, food and so on, so he starts pinching to help him meet his costs. And once he's started, he can't stop. It could be him, Aaron.'

Aaron shook his head. 'Nay, lad nowt's ever gone from his cloakroom. He does a good job for us, allus has.'

'So what are you going to do, Aaron?' asked Connolly, his eyes searching the old man's face as he mischievously put this question.

'T'committee's asked me to report the thefts to t'police, Mr Connolly. We did consider sacking Ada but felt we ought to be sure she was guilty first.'

'So you want us to catch Ada red-handed?'

'Well, aye, if that's what it means, Mr Connolly.'

'Right, we need a record of the crimes already committed; those you have recorded yourself will do for a start. Days, dates and times are what we need, with a list of things that have gone.'

Aaron had a list of those in his pocket, the result of the committee's interest in events. He handed them to Gerry, who scanned them.

'This'll do for us,' he said. 'I have to have evidence of the commission of the crimes before I can take action. Now, Aaron, how about a look around the hall?'

'Aye, any time.'

'Now?' he asked.

'Sure,' agreed Aaron. And so Gerry drove us to St Erasmus's Church Hall and let us in with his key. It was around 11.30 a.m. now, and the building was deserted.

The entrance was via two huge double doors in thick wood. They were painted a dark green and were as solid as those in ancient castles. They swung wide into a deep foyer, where on the left was the ladies' cloakroom, with the gentlemen's on the right. In each wall between the foyer and the cloakrooms was a hatch for handing over coats and other articles in return for tickets, while access to each cloakroom was a separate door leading from the foyer.

'Are the public allowed in at all?' I heard Connolly ask.

'Oh, aye,' acknowledged Aaron. 'Ah mean to say, Mr Connolly, the toilets are in there an' all, behind the coat rails. When a do is in progress, folks come and go all t' time. But Ada and Harry keep an eye on folks moving through. If anyone stopped to pick a pocket or raid a handbag, Ada would see 'em.'

'Even if she was coping with a rush of customers at that hatch? Issuing cloakroom tickets? Taking money?'

In Connolly's professional eyes, this was the first chink in the argument over Ada's probable guilt, but he looked carefully at the toilet, shut away in a cubicle behind the coat rails, and then had a look in the gentlemen's room. It mirrored the ladies' room.

'Now, Aaron,' he said, 'you said the stuff's been going during dances. So why dances, I wonder? What's the procedure at dances – by Ada and Harry, I mean?'

'Well, generally we start at eight or mebbe half-past, and we keep t'doors open till eleven. We never let anybody in after eleven; that's one of t'rules of this hall. After eleven, daft lads get stupid with drink and come causing bother, so we lock those outer doors till the dance ends. Folks can get out, sure, 'cos either Harry or

Ada'll unlocks t'doors, but nobody gets in after eleven. It doesn't matter whether it's a Saturday night dance that ends before midnight or a midweek 'un that goes on till one or two.'

Connolly asked, 'So Harry and Ada won't be taking coats after eleven?'

'No, but folks are using the toilets and they are dishing out coats to those who leave early – that's not many, mark you.'

'So what do Harry and Ada do after eleven?' asked Connolly.

'Relax a bit, Ah'd say,' said Aaron. 'Check t'takings, get ready for dishing t'coats out again, that sort o' thing.'

'Hmm,' he said. 'This is a puzzle, Aaron. Right, now I've seen the place, I'm going to put forward a suggestion. I'll need your consent, and I'll need total secrecy from you if you agree.'

Aaron looked at me for guidance, but I did not know what was in Gerry's mind.

'Aye, right, if it'll stop the pinching,' said Aaron.

'It'll tell us what goes on, but nobody must know we're operating here, right? Not even your committee.'

'Right, Mr Connolly.'

Gerry told him that a time-lapse camera would be installed in the ladies' cloakroom, and it would operate throughout the next dance and perhaps the one that followed. It took a picture every two seconds; it operated from a long-life battery and could be fixed to one of the wooden beams high above the cloakroom. It would be focused upon the rails of coats, and it had a wide-angle lens which would take in most of the floor area. If a thief came in to search the coats and handbags or to steal things like umbrellas and scarves, the camera would take a photograph of them in action.

'What about one in t'gents?' asked Aaron.

'We've only the one camera at the moment,' said Gerry. 'And it's in demand, as you can imagine. It's used almost exclusively for this kind of work.'

'So this sort o' thing goes on a lot, eh?' asked Aaron.

'It does, I'm afraid, Aaron. But now I'll need a note of the dates of your next few dances so we can select one when the camera is available. We'll start with the ladies.'

Aaron was in full agreement; for one thing, this would eliminate the necessity for a confrontation with Ada, and if she was guilty, this would provide proof instead of supposition.

Within a fortnight of that meeting, Gerry had obtained permission to make use of the camera, and the experts from Headquarters arrived to fit it. They were dressed in old overalls and came in an old van; if anyone saw them at work in the hall, the explanation was that they were inspecting the wiring on behalf of the council, a fairly routine examination.

Gerry and I went along to tell them exactly what was required of the camera, and a suitable place was determined. Happily, this hall had a lofty beamed ceiling without any form of underdrawing. Its rafters vanished into the darkness of the pointed roof. That applied to the cloakrooms too, and it was an easy task to conceal this small camera. It did make the tiniest of clicking sounds as it took its sequence of snaps, but it was felt the noise would not attract any interest – besides, no one could see into that dark roof void without a good torch, and the camera would be expertly sited and concealed.

The first dance at which our camera was to be a witness was scheduled for a Saturday night. At five o'clock I went to set the camera in motion; it would run for forty-eight hours if necessary, but our scenes-of-crime experts would return to the hall on Sunday morning to retrieve it. They, Gerry Connolly, Aaron and I would then inspect the developed pictures; they should be ready that same afternoon. Aaron's role was to identify any thief pictured on the film, and we knew he was dreading the task of having to identify Ada.

So the trap was set.

On the specific instructions of Sergeant Connolly, no police officers went into the dance hall that evening, although we were on duty in the office to await any call from Aaron. The uniform branch were not told of the reason for keeping away from the hall, but the instructions were issued via the duty sergeant, for we did not want our trap to be wasted by the unscheduled arrival of a crime-beating bobby. The dance progressed without incident until ten minutes to midnight, when a girl reported to Aaron, who was on duty as usual inside the main building, that her purse had been stolen, along with £5.12s.6d and a marcasite brooch worth 15 shillings.

Aaron took particulars, as he always did; in this he played a superb role, for he gave an absolutely normal response. After the dance hall had closed, he rang us with news of the latest theft, and we felt sure we must have captured the thief on film. We were all anxious to solve this one – was it Ada or not?

Although we had continued on duty until the end of the dance, just in case there had been other, unexpected developments, we now had to wait until Sunday to find out the truth about Ada Clarkson. On Sunday morning, the scenes-of-crime officers (SOCO) removed and developed the film. They came to Eltering Office at 3.30 p.m., when Aaron had been asked to attend.

'We've a good set,' beamed D/PC Mitchell as he addressed us. 'We've caught a woman in action, dipping into several pockets and purses, and we've got summat else.'

He spread the little black-and-white photographs along the table in sequence; each bore a date and time imprinted in white along the top edge.

'Right, this is the entrance to the cloakroom.' He indicated the door, standing open. 'These are the rails of coats, this is the chair where Mrs Clarkson sits to take money, and here, in the bottom left-hand corner, is the ladies' toilet with two cubicles. There's a door leading into each one, but we can't see into either because there's a roof over them.'

He began to point to each successive photograph and continued: 'At eleven-o-one and fifteen seconds, she goes out. That's when she locks the outer door, we believe. Comes back after twenty seconds ... see her? Leaves the cloakroom door open ... stands near the rails ... then, look at this! In comes lover boy ...'

'That's Harry!' cried poor old Aaron, in shock and some disbelief.

'Right,' said D/PC Mitchell. 'Harry comes into the ladies' cloakroom ... looks around ... goes to Ada ... they get into a clinch, see ... his hands are all over her ... and ... wait for it ... they go into one of the cubicles of the ladies' toilet and vanish from our sight. Both of 'em. Lock themselves in ... they were in there twenty bloody minutes ...'

'My God!' cried Aaron. 'Of all the people, of all the people I would never have said would do this ... adultery ... two people like that, two friends ... married ... happily ...'

'Hang on,' said Mitchell. 'Now, here comes your

thief.'

A young woman in her twenties came into the cloakroom as Ada and Harry were busy in the cubicle; she made a furtive entry, looked through the hatch to peer across the passage to see if Harry's cloakroom was empty, and then tried one cubicle door. It was locked, and so she tried the other – it was open and the cubicle was empty. At that point she began to rifle the pockets of the hanging coats. She worked through them quickly and expertly, and we could see her slipping items into her own handbag before leaving. In all, her actions took less than one minute, and no one else came in.

'Do you know her?' Connolly asked Aaron.

'Aye, it's that lass of Tomkins'. Jean.' He was still in a state of shock at the revelations about Ada. 'Works at the secondary modern school in the kitchens ... allus was a worry to her dad ... she's got a bairn, you know, not married, mind ...'

'Right, well, it looks as if we have found our thief.' Gerry was happy. 'Nick, you can interview her later today. Take a policewoman with you in case she says you tried to rape her. Get a cough, threaten to search her house for the other missing odds and sods ... get a voluntary from her.'

'Right, fine.' It would be nice to get several crimes written off as detected.

Connolly thanked Mitchell for the valuable use of the time-lapse camera and said its merits would be noted in his quarterly report to Headquarters. I was about to leave and interview Jean Tomkins when Aaron asked, 'Mr Connolly, that business between Ada and Harry. Well, I mean, what can I do now?'

'That is not a crime, Aaron. It's not an offence against criminal law, and so we are not interested. I'm afraid it's down to you.'

And so poor old Aaron had another matter about which to confront Ada Clarkson, and this time the police would not do it for him.

When I interviewed Jean Tomkins, she admitted more than twenty crimes she had committed in that cloakroom. And as an excuse, she said, 'I knew what Ada was up to, you see, and she's always at my mum for not going to church ...'

'You don't mean you did this to get at Ada?' I was astonished.

'I needed money, Mr Rhea, for my bairn. Ada was always pretending to be better than us, holier. Well, she's not, is she? Going into that toilet with Harry Nattrass, the dirty bitch ...'

It was odd hearing the girl speak like that; she seemed to think she was punishing Ada, whereas in reality she was punishing those from whom she had stolen.

Aaron did mention our findings to Ada and Harry, and they both left their work at the church hall. Ada also stopped going to church, but I don't think she stopped seeing Harry.

On another curious occasion we were asked to solve the problem of the disappearing bacon joints, and in this instance we also resorted to modern technology in our efforts to trace the thief.

The investigation began when we received a visit from a worried man called Brian King, who was manager of the bacon factory in Eltering. It was part of a large group of food wholesalers, and Brian, a local man in his late thirties, had been appointed manager some six months prior to this visit. Whatever the problems he had inherited, this one appeared to worry him deeply.

'I'd like advice,' he began, in what we had come to

learn was a familiar opening gambit.

'OK,' smiled Connolly, as charming as ever. 'What can we do for you, Mr King?'

'A member of my staff is thieving, Sergeant. Now, I'm sure you realise that it is putting a strain on me, but it is also throwing suspicion on every member of my workforce – that's almost thirty people, counting the office staff and drivers.'

'So, tell me, Mr King, how is this thief operating?'

'I don't know,' he sighed with the resignation of a defeated man. 'I've wracked my brains without coming to an answer, and I might add that I do have a very volatile workforce. If I make an accusation which I cannot substantiate, they will walk out; that would cost me my job.'

'We are not here to perform the duties of managers of business establishments, Mr King,' said Connolly, with more than a hint of firmness in his voice. 'Our job is to catch thieves, and if you make a formal complaint, we will do our best to achieve that. I'm afraid it might upset your staff if we start asking questions, but we can accept no responsibility for a deterioration in your manager/staff relationships.'

'I am aware of that, Sergeant, which is why I thought long and hard before coming to see you.'

'So long as we both understand that point. So, tell me, what is happening?'

'I did wonder whether some secret method might be employed first; one reads of devices that will photograph a thief or those powders that will leave traces on their hands if they touch an object which has been marked ...'

'Yes, we do have such facilities,' smiled Connolly, 'but, in fairness, I would guess a factory would be too large an area for our time-lapse camera to be of any use and, well, to paint all your bits of meat with fluorescent powder might not be feasible ... I've no idea what it would do to the meat, for example ...'

'But you will help me?'

'If you are making a formal complaint of a series of thefts in your establishment, then, yes, we will come along and sort it out.'

King took a deep breath and nodded fiercely. 'Yes, I will make a formal complaint, and to hell with the consequences.'

'Good,' beamed Connolly. 'Then let's hear your story.'

King told us that for the past few weeks small joints of top-quality bacon had been spirited out of the factory. At first it was thought the checking system was faulty, but a careful check on the stock did reveal a deficiency over each week. Five or six joints were being taken each week. It was not a lot, he stressed. It was not as if drivers or delivery men were filching lorry loads of meat or the workers somehow fiddling massive sides of bacon, hams or half-pigs. The stolen objects were joints of dressed bacon, small enough to hide under an overall or even in a cycle saddlebag. They weighed two or three pounds and were highly popular with people living alone, and with pensioners.

'When are they disappearing?' I asked, for I was involved with this enquiry in my capacity as Aide.

'At night, almost every night,' he said, wringing his hands. 'We prepare the meat each morning, freshly killed, of course, and a lot goes out the same day. But some we dress during the afternoons, then place it in a cool room overnight. Some we freeze, of course, and some we place in chilled accommodation – a refrigerator. But not these joints – there's a high turnover of them, they're one of our best lines, and so they are laid out ready to be loaded into our vans first thing the next morning. Each morning our vans go out into the town, or into neighbouring towns and villages, to sell those products. There are other small items too – sausages, pork pies, sliced bacon, liver and so on. But only those joints are stolen.'

'So they vanish after you lock up at night and before you open next morning? What times are those?' I asked.

'We close at 4.30 p.m. and we open next morning at 6 a.m.'

'Any sign of forced entry?' asked Connolly.

'No, that's one of my worries. I think the thief has a key; we've thought about changing the locks, but I don't think head office would sanction that expenditure, especially for such a reason.'

'You've asked them?' Connolly put to him.

'Er, no, not yet. It would be a last resort.'

'So, am I right in thinking all your staff are now under suspicion?'

'Yes, I'm afraid so. It's not as if it's a major series of thefts, Sergeant, but, if someone is getting away with those joints at the rate of five or six a week, they are making a useful extra income, at our expense. And my workforce are now beginning to distrust one another ...'

'You've discussed it with them?'

'Yes, without my suggesting one of them is a thief. But they now wonder which of them is the pilferer ... they're an honest crowd, you see, Sergeant, but there is a definite air of unease in the factory. I must bring things to a conclusion.'

He told us that several members of staff had keys and that the keys were of the old-fashioned mortise type, so easy to copy and even make. Security seemed very lax, we felt.

'Do any members of staff know of your visit to us?' asked Connolly.

'Only my secretary,' he said. 'And she can be trusted. I asked her not to disclose my whereabouts.'

'Right,' said Connolly. 'Before we can go any further, we need to inspect your factory. When would be suitable?'

'Any evening, Sergeant,' he said.

Gerry Connolly was of the opinion that there was no time like the present, and we agreed to meet Mr King at the factory that night at eight o'clock. At the appointed time, he met us in the car park, let us in and showed us around. The place was well lit at night, and it comprised a series of large rooms, some used for preparation and some for storage.

At the side of the building was the office block. We toured the entire complex, examining doors and windows, noting that there were several skylights which were kept open, as were several high windows, especially in the factory portion. These were high enough off the ground to be beyond the reach of children. Some around the lower parts of the walls were also kept open, but stoutly barred. No fully grown man or woman could wriggle through.

'A duplicate key job, it seems to me,' said Connolly, partly to me and partly to himself. 'A sneak thief with inside knowledge, one who's prepared to let all his or her colleagues be suspected. We'll have to nail the bastard, Nick.'

The cold room in which the joints of bacon were laid out in readiness for morning had no windows, although it did have a gap where the door should be. There was no door; access was via a corridor, itself kept almost at freezing-point, with fridges and deep-freezes along its way. Once inside the factory, anyone could run along this corridor, snaffle a joint and leave.

'Right,' said Gerry, having seen the premises. 'We'll use a pressure mat.'

'What's that?' asked King.

'It is a pad of rubber which fits beneath a door mat or rug, or even a carpet for that matter. It bleeps when someone stands on it. There is a door mat outside that cold room of yours, so this won't be noticed.'

'Won't it alert the thief if it bleeps?' asked King.

'No,' smiled Gerry. 'We pop the pressure mat under the existing door mat, and it is plugged into the electrical circuit. Inside, there is a bleeper, but it doesn't sound in the premises; it sounds in a police car outside, or in a police station. When it bleeps, we surround the place and arrest the villain because we know he's inside.'

'It sounds perfect,' said King.

'It isn't,' said Connolly. 'Some villains move so fast that they're off the premises before we can get in, but it has had a lot of success.'

'I'd like you to try it, please. You have my approval.'

And so we prepared our trap.

On the first night, the bleeper sounded and we rushed to the factory, but he had gone before we arrived. And so had a joint of bacon. On the second night, the same thing happened, except that in this instance we were waiting outside, only a minute away by car. There was no sign of a break-in during any of these raids. We dare not reveal our presence immediately outside the factory in case we alerted our suspect, but when he escaped on the third night, without even a sighting by the waiting police officers, we decided we must take alternative action. Could someone actually hide in the factory? The timing

161

of each raid did vary slightly, although most were between 10 p.m. and midnight. A two-hour wait in those chilly rooms was not the finest of ways of spending an evening, and yet it seemed the only answer.

We drew straws. I drew the short one.

'Right, Nick. You're first on. Wrap up in your warmest clothes and wait in that cold room. We'll re-set the pressure mat so that it bleeps the moment someone stands on it; at that sound, switch on your torch to highlight the thief – he'll be in the doorway at that time, and then switch on all the lights in the factory. We'll have men outside all the doors to nab him as he runs out.'

That night, therefore, I wrapped in layers of long johns and sweaters and put on furry boots, the sort we used when on winter patrol, and prepared for my stint. I let myself in with a key provided by Mr King and had no trouble finding my way along the corridor to the cold room. I saw the mat and avoided standing on it as I entered the chill room with its complement of prepared bacon joints. They filled several tables and shelves around the roof. There seemed to be hundreds ... And then I settled down to a long, cold wait.

Later, in the chilling darkness, I heard a slight noise. It was a noise which I could not identify, and the hair on the nape of my neck prickled and stood erect as I waited. My heart began to thump as I knew someone was approaching, so silently, so carefully ... I wished I had a colleague with me; I wished someone else had drawn that short straw ... and then silence. Nothing. I dare not move now. Had I been detected? Had the thief spotted the pressure mat? There was no light, so I assumed he had not.

And then the bleep. It made me jump with fright, it

was so sudden, but there it was. The thief was in the room now, there with me, and so I switched on my torch. Immediately the room was filled with light, and I saw the distinct figure of a young fox running off with a bacon joint.

'Hey!' I shouted, giving chase and hitting the first light switch I found. But he galloped along that corridor and leapt onto a window ledge, squeezed through the bars of the open window with the joint between his teeth and jumped onto the branch of a tree outside. And then he vanished.

The outer door burst open and in charged Sergeant Connolly and a couple of uniformed policemen. 'Where is he?'

'Gone,' I said. 'Got clean away.'

'Nick, you don't mean that ...' Gerry sounded more sorry than angry. 'You mean you sat in there and let him get away ...'

'Sergeant,' I said, 'if you're going to catch this thief, you'll need more than a handful of policemen.'

'Rubbish!' He was still rising to my bait. 'Look, Nick, this is not good enough. I should have put a more experienced detective in here.'

'No, Sarge,' I laughed. 'You should have put a Master of Foxhounds and a pack of good dogs. The thief is a fox. He got away through that window.'

'You're joking,' he smiled.

'I'm not,' I said. 'Sharp as lightning, he was; he knows he can just get a joint between those bars ...'

'Who's going to tell Mr King?' He looked at us all.

'You are, Sergeant,' we all chanted.

Chapter 9

For God's sake, look after our people.
ROBERT FALCON SCOTT (1868-1912)

OF THE VARIETY OF events in the police officer's calendar, that of a visit by a Very Important Person is often the most fraught, because the personage must be protected against madmen and terrorists and at the same time proceed along a predestined route without interruption. To permit the populace to see and even speak to the personage and at the same time prevent lunatics shooting them or throwing rotten eggs into their faces is not the most easy of tasks. But the work of the VIP must be allowed to continue, and the VIP in question must not allow the less sane members of society to hinder their freedom and their communion with ordinary folk.

In understanding the risks that prevail each time a member of the royal family or a top politician appears in public, I have the greatest admiration for them. They can never go out alone, not even into the shops or to an inn for a drink; they are always surrounded by an army of officials, and they can never drop their guard for one tiniest moment. They have no privacy, and their every word and action is scrutinised, criticised and headlined in the less savoury of our newspapers.

The movements of VIPs are of concern to the police because a police constable holds office under the sovereign. He or she is an officer of the Crown and also a public servant, and the constable's duty includes the protection of life and property, whether that life and property belong to a VIP or not. That is a wide brief, but it does include the protection of important people as well as the protection of ordinary mortals, amongst whom the constable himself can be numbered. Constables are ordinary people who are charged with extraordinary powers and responsibilities.

But obviously there are occasions when a Very Important Person requires more attention than usual. A visit by HM The Queen to a local town is such an occasion, but does this also include the opening of a new supermarket by a well-known TV personality? Exactly what is a Very Important Person?

A lot of people think themselves important for reasons which are sometimes quite strange. Because some have grown rich or famous, they feel they are important, and because some have become personalities via television, they also feel themselves important. But are they? The snag is that famous singers or entertainers can draw crowds, and so the police must then act to prevent obstructions and danger to the public when these people manifest themselves in public places. The fact that a bunch of scruffy youths can sing in a way that appeals to teenagers does give them some importance, if only because they are an utter nuisance when they move around the globe. It is important that they do not get in the way of others trying to go about their business.

Being a police officer does allow one to work closely with VIPs, if only in a protective sense, and there are many duties which the service must perform when a VIP visits the area. The obvious ones are control of traffic and crowds, and the less obvious ones involve security and planning. When Her Majesty visits, however, there is more planning and more security because there are greater crowds and more traffic, coupled with the continuing risk to her life. Every movement is planned to the minute, every step she takes is arranged in advance and rehearsed, and every possible security measure is taken. A royal visit is a headache to the security services and the police, and when it concludes without incident, there is immense satisfaction and immense relief.

But things can go wrong. There was one famous occasion when Her Majesty's motorcade was cruising through a northern town. All routes had been sealed off, including a tiny back alley which led directly onto the royal route. But at the crucial moment the constable whose duty was to halt traffic at that exit was called to an elderly lady who had collapsed in the crowd. As no traffic was waiting in his alley, he attended the old lady. Any right-minded person would have done likewise.

And then, just as the royal procession was approaching, a dustcart chugged down that alley and emerged directly ahead of the motorcade. Before anyone could prevent it, the dustcart, with grimy men hanging on to it and the effluvium of the town's waste accompanying it, had become part of the procession. It was behind the leading police motor-cycle outriders but in front of the royal limousine. And there was no way off that route for over a mile. To enthusiastic cheers from the townspeople, their dustcart preceded the royal procession until a convenient layby materialised; it was then gently guided out of Her Majesty's way. I'm sure she was amused.

It is that kind of mishap that causes senior police officers to worry about their pensions, for all dread the likelihood of something going wrong, especially during a royal visit.

I remember when Prince Charles came to Strensford as part of the town's 1,300th anniversary celebrations of its abbey's foundation. The great unveiling of a plaque was about to occur. The local brass band was waiting to play. As His Royal Highness and other dignitaries stood by, with Prince Charles waiting to perform the unveiling ceremony, the bishop began his eulogy. His speech was timed to continue for twenty minutes, but he made the mistake of pausing after the first paragraph. Bishops seem to enjoy long, meaningful pauses, but this one was too long for the conductor of the brass band; he thought the bishop had finished. He promptly brought his musicians to life, and their rumbustious music shortened that ceremony by a good quarter of an hour.

Prince Charles was amused and, I think, relieved, for he later said to the conductor, 'You came in there a bit quick, eh?' and chuckled.

But surely the worst experience to have occurred in our force was when I was an Aide to the CID at Strensford. Somehow, a combination of events managed to lose Her Majesty The Queen.

The intelligent reader will ask: how on earth can anyone lose the Queen?

It happened like this.

Her Majesty had a very important engagement in London one evening, one which could not be cancelled. It was scheduled to finish around 9 p.m. But she also had an equally important engagement in Edinburgh at 10 a.m. the following morning. She therefore decided to travel by royal train, leaving London at 10 p.m. with her entourage. She would sleep on the train, and it was decided that the royal train would break its journey around midnight, when it would be guided into a quiet, peaceful and secure siding until around 7.30 a.m., when it would resume its journey, to arrive in Edinburgh around 9.30 a.m., in good time for Her Majesty's 10 a.m. engagement. Thus the royal train would be parked somewhere for about seven hours. That place had to be secure, private and yet accessible to the main London-Edinburgh route. And what better place than a tiny branch line on the north-eastern edge of the North York Moors?

It was therefore decreed that the royal train would be diverted off the main line and through some scenic countryside which embraced the branch line that led from Thirsk into the hills. The line passed through the villages of Little Cringle, Harksworth and Crossby before regaining the main line some fifteen miles to the north. The Beeching Axe closed this line in 1964, but the tracks were still there, and it was ideal for this purpose.

The royal train would remain overnight in Little Cringle Station, which stood a mile or so from the village after which it was named, and it was the duty of our police force to provide security and protection to the train and its VIP passengers during its stay. I was one of the CID men detailed for that duty, one of several, in fact. My role was to arrive at Little Cringle Station at 11.30 p.m. and remain there on security duties until departure of the train next morning. The royal train was expected to arrive at 12.35 a.m.

Armed with my flask of coffee and a box of sandwiches, I drove through the dark lanes to Little Cringle and reported to the sergeant in charge at the deserted station. I was posted to a bridge overlooking the line, and had to stop anarchists and their ilk from dropping bombs onto the royal train. I had no firearm, only my detective stave and a personal radio. I hoped the anarchists would never know that.

And so, that fine May night, I walked up and down that bridge, waiting for the train to appear. The expected time of arrival passed with no sign of it. Another half an hour passed and still there was no sign, and I could see my colleagues on the station moving around in concern.

Clearly, there was a problem of some kind, for trains with the Queen on board should never be late. I knew I must not leave my post without good reason, and so I walked up and down, puzzled and growing increasingly concerned as time passed without any reports. Then the detective sergeant came to me, walking quickly through the night.

'Nick,' he said, 'we've a problem. Come into the office.'

I followed him into the disused station master's office which had been utilised as a control room for this occasion, and found the others sitting around.

'Right,' said Detective Sergeant Proctor. 'We're all here, and this is the problem. The royal train should have arrived here at 12.35 a.m. and it hasn't. It has Her Majesty on board and members of her entourage, including her private police officer. I have checked with British Rail and our own control room, and they maintain the train is where it should be. They say it is here. Well, I for one know it bloody well isn't. You all know that it isn't here, and you can't just spirit away an engine and several coaches full of VIPs. We have a radio link with the train, of course, and the chap on duty says the train is in its siding, safe and sound, and Her Majesty is sleeping. He reckons he is at Little Cringle as arranged, and he will not accept any other suggestion. And the main line is clear, gentlemen, so the royal train is not on the main line. British Transport police have

169

checked.'

'Then where the hell is it?' asked one of the detectives.

'We don't know. The signalman at Thirsk, whose job was to switch the points for it to enter this line, has gone off duty. We're having a man sent to have words with him, to see if he's diverted it along the wrong bloody line – either by design or by carelessness.'

That this might have been done deliberately presented a chilling scenario and had horrific implications for the effectiveness of the overall security arrangements surrounding Her Majesty.

'But if the chap in charge of the train thinks he's at Little Cringle, or *says* he's at Little Cringle, something is wrong.' I had my little say. 'Could the royal train have got into the wrong hands?'

'Oh, for God's sake don't start thinking like that!' groaned the sergeant. 'It's bad enough losing the bloody train, let's not start thinking somebody's kidnapped the Queen! This isn't a bloody novel, Nick, it's real life!'

'It must have got shunted into the wrong branch line,' concluded Proctor. 'It's the only possible answer. Now, who's got the map?'

Someone produced an Ordnance Survey map of the district which the CID had used to identify which bridges to supervise and which roads to patrol, and Proctor examined it. After a moment, he said, 'Nick, here a minute. This is your patch, isn't it?'

He indicated a branch line which led from just south of Thirsk and through the hills into Ryedale, reaching the villages of Maddleskirk and Elsinby, both on my own beat.

'It's not used by service trains, Sergeant,' I told him. 'But it is used occasionally. Maddleskirk College do have trains visiting Maddleskirk Station to deliver boys to the college. Special trains come at the start of each term and at the end of each term. The line is still open, but there's no public service now, no through trains.'

As he spoke, a radio call came from Headquarters. It was to say that an officer had visited the home of the signalman in question, but he was not there. His mother said he'd only been doing the job for a few weeks and that he'd come home, got changed and gone fishing. He was a keen fisherman and hadn't gone to bed because he now had two days off and wanted to make full use of them. She had no idea where he'd gone; he rarely told her. She did say that he usually went up Swaledale, but he might have gone over into Eskdale looking for salmon, or there again he might have gone to Whitby to do some sea fishing from a boat. The message also said that, whatever line the train had been sent along, its points had now reverted to their original position to cater for main-line expresses, and so no one knew which line had been used. We put an All-Stations message out for all police officers to seek this signalman; he had to be interviewed without delay.

'Right, Nick, I'm going to send you over to Maddleskirk. It'll take you, what? Half-an-hour from here? Check that line, will you, and see if you can find the royal train. I'll have checks made on the other lines – there's lots branch off the main line between York and Darlington. Yours is the one immediately before the one that should have been utilised; that signalman could have pulled the wrong lever.'

And so I went about my mission. But when I got to Maddleskirk Station, which, like the one at Little Cringle, lies a mile out of the village, there was no sign of a train. I motored through the valley to Elsinby and again found no sign of a train, but then, at the tiny halt beyond Elsinby at Ploatby Junction, I could see the dark bulk of a stationary train. Ploatby Junction was not really a station, only a mere halt where, in the past, the line divided. One branch extended from here to Malton, while the other went into Ashfordly. Now it was unmanned and unused; there was not even a sign to announce its name. I drove steadily along the land and parked on the ashen surface which had once been a car park. There was no one around, although one of the carriages of the still train did bear dim lights.

I went towards that carriage, noting it was now 2.15 a.m. I tapped on the door, hoping to God it did not contain the Queen's apartments, and it was opened by a smart-suited man with close-cropped hair.

'What is it?' he snapped.

'CID,' I said, producing my warrant card. 'D/PC Rhea, local force.'

'Come in, and don't slam the door,' he said.

I went in and found myself in a mobile office; he gave me a mug of steaming coffee and then asked, 'Where the hell have your lot been? We've been here the best part of a couple of hours with never a sign of any liaison ... talk about security ...'

'You're in the wrong station,' I said. 'This is not Little Cringle, this is Ploatby Junction.'

'You're not serious? Have we passed Cringle?'

'No. You're not on the right line,' I said. 'You've been sent down the wrong branch line ...'

'My God! Is this line busy? Hell, if something runs into us ...'

'No, no problem,' I told him. 'It's disused, it's quite safe, there's no traffic on this line at night,' and I explained things to him.

'My God, trust British Rail! So what do we do now?'

'I suggest you remain here till morning,' I said. 'It's safe, you can be back on the main line within a few minutes, although you'll have to reverse all the way, and you can be on your way on time tomorrow without any problems.' I explained the geography of the district to him with the aid of a map in his mobile office.

'I'll check with BR and suggest that. You know, when your lot said we were on the wrong line, we thought it could be somebody breaking in to your wavelengths, somebody out to harm Her Majesty. From leaving the main line, the time it took us to arrive here was just the same as if we'd gone to Little Cringle. We saw this platform and halted, just as normal. Mind, I did find it odd that no one from the local *gendarmerie* came to liaise with us.'

'I'd better radio Headquarters and tell them where you are,' I said.

And so I did. The detectives from Little Cringle all rushed over to Ploatby Junction, and we adopted our guardian role from that point onwards. At 7.25 a.m. the driver started his engine, and the huge train slowly reversed towards the distant main line, where another signalman had come on duty. Her Majesty and her entourage had had a pleasant night's sleep, totally unaware that they had spent the night in an unscheduled location and blissfully unaware of our alarm.

I arrived home just as Mary was getting up and dressing the family. I stayed out of bed and helped and then had my breakfast with my wife and little family of four children.

'Did you have a busy night?' asked Mary when we had time to chat.

'I was involved in the royal visit to Ploatby,' I said,

but I don't think she believed the Queen had slept within sight of our lofty police house.

I wondered how that tiny community of two or three farms and a dozen or so houses at Ploatby would have reacted if they had known that Her Majesty had spent the night among them.

Later the rumours did begin to circulate, and one of the local men said to me, 'Noo then, Mr Rhea, Ah've 'eard tell that Her Majesty had ti sleep on yon station t'other week. Now, there's no fire there, no waiting-room, no toilets, nowhere for a cup o' tea or a sandwich. Nowt. Noo, if Ah'd known that, she could have used my bed for t'night – Ah'd have moved out, tha knows, if they'd come and asked. T'sheets wad have been warmed up and we've allus got eggs and bacon in for breakfast. It's nut right, is it, letting a Queen sleep on a draughty station like that when there's folks here wi' spare beds and spare rooms?'

'I'll pass the word on in case it happens again,' I promised him. In fact, it did happen again, for before the tracks were removed, this line was considered ideal for parking the royal train at night. But I don't think any of its passengers enjoyed bed-and-breakfast in Ploatby.

Another VIP visit caused a bit of a flutter in Aidensfield. I learned of it through a chat with George, the landlord of the Brewers' Arms.

'I'm not sure whether this is a matter for you or not,' he said, 'but we've a famous person coming to the pub for dinner next week. Friday night.'

'Is he staying at the Brewers' Arms?' I asked.

'No. He's just coming for dinner. He's arriving with Sir Eldric and Lady Tippet-Greve, and they have requested total secrecy. They do not want his visit spoiled by sightseers, and they have sworn me to total secrecy.'

'Is it a politician or a member of the royal family?' I asked. 'We don't normally take an interest in visits by those who are not in that category.'

'No, he's a singer,' said George. 'He's staying with Sir Eldric and Lady Tippet-Greve at High Hall for five days. He's doing a spot of grouse-shooting on the moors and wants to see something of North York Moors and the scenery. And he wants to see a typical English pub, to have a pint and a meal there.'

'So they're bringing him to the Brewers' Arms, eh?' I smiled. 'Well, they couldn't find a better example of a village pub, George. You'll feed him well?'

'There's a party of a dozen coming,' said George. 'I'm having the dining-room decorated for the job, but I thought I'd better tell you, just in case we get trouble in the village.'

'If no one knows he's coming, George, I think things will pass peacefully on Friday.'

'Aye, but word gets around, you know; I mean, once he's inside, folks'll recognise him and they'll be ringing their friends and they'll come to the pub, and before we know it, there'll be chaos.'

'I'm on an attachment to CID, George,' I said. 'I'll have to get another uniformed constable to pay a visit.'

'No, no,' he said. 'I don't want that, I don't want anyone outside Aidensfield to know he's coming. If a uniformed bobby hangs about, folks will sense there's something going on. Can't you come in civvies, off duty? Just to be around, just in case? Their tables are booked for eight. They've taken the whole dining-room.'

It was an earnest plea and, as I was not anticipating having to work that evening, I said, 'I'll see what I can do, George, but I really ought to know who's coming.

Just in case.'

'You won't tell a soul, will you?' he pleaded. 'I mean, I could get into a load of bother if word gets out.'

'It's our secret, George,' I assured him.

'It's Bing Crosby!' he said. 'Bing Crosby's coming to the Brewers' Arms!'

I knew this would not present the kind of problems one associated with the Beatles or the Rolling Stones, but if word did reach the wider public, there could be a crowd and there could be problems that were associated with crowds. There might be traffic congestion in the village, and if some wilder elements came along, there could be trouble such as minor fights and the kind of bother one expects from silly youths, especially if they resort to drinking on the street. I also knew George wasn't imagining this, for it had been reported that 'The Old Groaner' was in the area on a private visit.

He was not performing at any concerts, and the entire visit was being regarded as a personal and private one. Until now, I'd had no idea he was acquainted with the Tippet-Greves.

'I'll be there,' I promised George.

In the days that followed, everyone in Aidensfield and district heard the news, and when I arrived at the pub with Mary (in whom I had confided the secret), I found it packed. People who never normally patronised the Brewers' Arms were there, old ladies with glazed eyes were there, youngsters who had heard about Crosby and weren't quite sure what he did were there, and everyone was struggling to buy drinks at the bar and to catch a glimpse of the crooner.

'He got here early,' said George to me in a confidential whisper. 'Sir Eldric's party is in the dining-room. We've drawn the curtains for privacy.'

'Thanks. A good idea,' I agreed, for it was almost dark anyway, being a late September day. By this time, a small crowd had gathered outside, hoping to catch sight of Crosby, but his early arrival had defeated them. It was a pity, I felt, for they were local people who were simply standing there to catch a sight of this world-famous singer. Inside, however, the place was packed. I moved among the crowd, fighting for space as Mary chatted to some friends, fans of Crosby, who had heard the whispered rumours. A couple of hours passed in this way, and then George hailed me.

'There's a coach arrived!' he said. 'In the car park at the back. I can't cope with a coach-load of fans, Nick. Can you send 'em on their way?'

'I'll have words with them,' I assured him.

I went into the car park at the rear of the inn and saw a crowd of men descending from a mini-bus, a twelve-seater. Others joined them from a couple of cars parked behind. There'd be twenty men in all. But no coach.

I had to be diplomatic, for I was not wearing uniform, and besides, I could not ban these men from the Brewers' Arms. I had no such power. Besides, a too-forceful attempt to deter them would only result in their determination to find out why.

'It's full, gents!' I said. 'Packed out. You'll never reach the bar.'

'Want a bet, mister?' grinned one of them. 'We don't play rugger for nothing. We can always make a scrum. Thanks, but we'll get our pints. We'll be no trouble if we're left alone.'

And they marched steadfastly across the car park to the back door of the inn. As they did so, a little man carrying a pork-pie hat emerged and walked towards me. I waited in the car park, watching the departing rugger team as they filed, one by one, into the packed inn. I hoped they would not cause bother – I could always ring for a duty car if bother was threatened.

The rugger team passed the little man, and he seemed lost as he noticed me standing in the centre of the car park.

'Say,' he said in that soft and most distinctive voice, 'where's the john?'

'It's a bit primitive,' I said jokingly. 'A relic of the last century.'

'I don't care,' he chuckled. 'Gee, I am enjoying this.'

'It is Mr Crosby, isn't it?' I ventured.

'Sure, but without my toupee, no one knows me; I just walked through that crowd in there, and no one stopped me. You won't tell, will you?'

'No, of course not. I'm the village policeman, by the way, PC Rhea.'

'Glad to know you. I like this village, Mr Rhea, and your countryside. Marvellous, but I must hurry. My hosts'll wonder where I've got to.'

He went into the unlit toilet, a brick-built square which had a urinal channel and a battered water closet in a separate cubicle. But there was no light, and the only ventilation was via the open top of the affair, for it had no roof.

I returned to Mary, and as I was talking, Crosby came back into the hotel, pushed past the crowds and reached me. He recognised me.

'Sure is a quaint john,' he said quietly, chuckling as he moved back into the dining-room without anyone recognizing him.

'Who's that?' asked my pal Malcolm.

'Bing Crosby,' I said.

'Never ... I don't believe that ...'

'He's taken his toupee off,' I told him. 'He likes not being recognised, and he looks smaller than he does on screen ...'

'But I wanted to meet him ...'

'You nearly did,' I grinned.

And then the rugger team started to sing. Word of our illustrious guest had reached them, and they launched into 'White Christmas' with all the fervour a rugger team can muster. I groaned, and I could see that George was angry and upset at their behaviour.

'Shut up!' I heard him appeal to them. 'We don't want the evening spoilt ...'

But they continued in fine voice, doing a repertoire of Crosby's songs, and George was growing more and more embarrassed. The more he tried to persuade them to end their singing, the more determined they became to sing, and we felt sure their music would reach the ears of the party in the dining-room. George decided to apologise to Sir Eldric and his party, and went across to the dining-room. At least no one was hanging around outside its door. I watched from the distance, and then George came out, closely followed by Crosby.

Crosby came into the bar and stood behind the counter with George, who rapped for silence.

'Quiet, everybody!' George's loud voice filled the bar, and he rapped it again with an ashtray. Even the rugger team fell silent.

'Ladies and gentlemen,' he shouted, for there was still a babble of excited chatter at the appearance of Crosby at his side, 'Mr Bing Crosby.'

The pub filled with cheers as Crosby said, 'I've enjoyed my visit to your inn.' We all cheered again. 'And so I thought I'd join your choir with a few songs...'

And so he did. Led by Bing Crosby, the combined choirs of the Vale of Mowbray 1st XV, the regulars of the Brewers' Arms and a handful of visitors from surrounding villages sang a medley of the best-known Crosby songs led by the maestro himself. And we ended by singing 'White Christmas'.

Crosby had to leave with his party but he had given us a fine concert, and George bought drinks for everyone that night, even for the visiting rugger team. Two or three weeks later a signed photograph of Crosby arrived, and it was placed in a position of distinction behind the bar.

But perhaps the best news of all came a month or two later. George showed me the letter he had received from the brewery which owned the premises.

It announced that new indoor toilets for ladies and gents were to be installed.

People who consider themselves important, but who are probably not in the least meritorious, often find themselves in situations which are embarrassing. A lot of this is due to their opinion of themselves, some believing they are God's gift to the world and that, as a consequence, nothing they do is wrong, while others blithely jog along in the erroneous view that they are indispensable to the nation which has nurtured them. To be very well known is indeed a severe handicap. That became evident in this next tale.

Such a person was a Very Famous TV Personality. I am not allowed to name him here, nor even to create a fictitious name which might, with some astute detective work, lead to his identification. And so I will call him VFTVP – Very Famous TV Personality.

That he was talented, handsome and popular was never in doubt, but it was known to those closely associated with him that his desirability and attractiveness concealed a person who was not very nice at all. The police in whose area he lived knew of his peccadilloes and of his more serious wrongdoings, one of which was a conviction for rape when he was a teenage lout.

His appearances on the screens of our national television network had made him a modern household name, and those of us who knew of his background and of his seedy private life sometimes wondered how the public would react if they knew the truth about him. But we, as police officers, could never reveal a confidence of that kind. We knew about his past, and we respected his efforts to forge a new future.

As part of his new image, he had married a delightful young actress, and the publicity shots of them together in their current bliss did seem to suggest he had reformed. Certainly, it made the old ladies and the middle-aged ladies who were his chief fans think he was wonderful, kind, considerate and generally quite charming. But we knew he was an out-and-out bastard, a womanizing drunkard, and that he beat his wife without mercy. Time and time again our men had been called to the cottage he rented on the Moors to quell the violent disputes he created at his home. And then, next morning, he would be his usual charming self.

Oddly enough, one of his fans was D/PC Wharton, with whom I worked in Eltering CID. He had seen the programmes that featured the VFTVP, and we knew that he modelled himself on the man. The clothes, the hair-do and even some of the jargon he used had come from the screen image of that appalling man. He knew of the rape conviction but reckoned that the worst of men could be reformed and redeemed. And that is what he felt about our VFTVP. It required a murder investigation to change his mind.

The body of a woman had been found in woodland close to Eltering, and she had been strangled. Her clothes had been scattered around the area, she had been savagely raped and her life had ended with her own tights being tied around her neck. She was twenty-four years old and the daughter of a local racehorse trainer.

The body was found at four o'clock one August afternoon, and we managed to keep the news of the discovery out of the regional TV and news programmes; it would be released at nine o'clock in readiness for blanket coverage in the following day's newspapers. Our aim was not to deny news to the public but to try to trap her killer.

We reckoned that lack of news that evening would compel the killer to return to the scene, just to see if his handiwork had been discovered. Several of us were therefore detailed to keep observations in that forest. I found myself doing the 8-10 p.m. stint with Paul Wharton. Our mission was simple – we had to conceal ourselves in the forest so that we could overlook the patch of land where the body had been discovered. As a forest track passed between that patch and our hiding place, we had also to note the registration numbers and descriptions of cars which passed along that route.

There were no incidents of major interest until at almost 9.30 p.m., a Rover 2000 eased to a halt outside our patch of forest. We could see it contained two people, a man and a woman. Then it reversed into the trees. It moved along a wide track covered with pine needles, and we could see the two people talking for a few minutes, and then they climbed out and got into the rear seat. There were further animated movements of arms, lots of kissing and passion and then, with a scream, the woman flung open the car door and ran into the trees, her clothing torn and flying behind.

The man ran after her, shouting obscenities which rang through the woodland as the girl was calling, 'No, don't, no ...'

'Time for Sir Galahad to rescue a fair maid, you think?' said Wharton.

'You take the girl, I'll get him,' I said, more in hope than expectation.

Wharton ran. We did not need torches in the half-light, and as I galloped to head off the chasing man, he called after the girl, 'It's all right, it's the police ...'

I was closing on the man with great speed, for it was clear that he was physically out of condition. When I was behind him, I called for him to halt, but he refused. He was clearly terrified of me and Paul Wharton, not knowing what he had let himself in for.

'Police!' I shouted as I closed in. 'Halt ...'

He replied with a stream of abuse, and so I accelerated over those closing yards and brought him down with a flying rugby tackle. We crashed head first into the soft carpet of pine needles, his body acting as a cushion for mine as I knocked the wind out of him. I picked him up and snapped my handcuffs on him before he could do any more harm, then held his manacled arms as I steered him back to his own Rover. He never spoke during that walk. As I approached the car, I saw that Paul had caught the girl and they were walking back together, Paul supporting her with his arms.

'So,' said Paul as my man sank against the car for support, 'what's all this?'

'He tried to rape me, that's what! I know I agreed to a cuddle and a spot of music on the radio, but he went berserk.'

'She led me on, I thought she was game ...' and the face turned around to reveal his identity. It was our VFTVP.

'I did no such thing, you evil bastard ...' she bellowed at him. 'You are filthy, you are evil, you want locking up ...'

Paul, his dreams shattered, was horrified. 'But it's ... you are ...'

'Sod off, you stupid copper!' snapped the VFTVP. 'I want my solicitor. This cow is a prostitute ... I've paid her to come here tonight ... I'll ruin her in court, so help me ...'

'I'm not, I'm not, I thought you loved me!' wept the girl.

'You are under arrest for attempted rape,' said Paul, his face as grim as the granite rocks which surrounded us. 'You are not obliged to say anything unless you wish to do so, but what you say may be taken down in writing and given in evidence.'

'That bitch is a slut, a cow and a pro. Put that in your notebooks and see if I care.'

We radioed our control room to report this arrest and, in view of the fame of our prisoner, were told to take him to the Divisional Headquarters, where a detective chief inspector would interview him.

For Paul Wharton, there had been the shattering of an illusion, and he no longer believed in the truth of screen images. For me, there was disappointment too. In spite of what we had witnessed, we could not proceed against the VFTVP because the girl refused to make a formal complaint and declined to be a witness. This case occurred many years before the anonymity procedures which now protect victims and suspects alike, and the girl did not want her name dragging through the courts and newpapers. She did not want to be regarded as a loose woman, a slag, a prostitute or a rich man's plaything. And so we could not prosecute him – besides, it was a very doubtful case of attempted rape anyway. We might have secured a conviction for indecent assault – but we got nothing.

For the general public and all his thousands of adoring fans, the VFTVP continued to charm those who saw him in action on their screens. None knew of his darker side but I did learn, two or three years later, that some of the tabloid press were quietly investigating his life-style and were compiling a dossier. One day, I felt, all would be revealed.

And for the detective chief inspector, there was hope.

'I think he killed that lass,' he said to me many days later. 'That story told by your girl, about him ripping off her clothes and so on, well, it all fits with the murdered lass.'

'Did you ask him about his whereabouts at the time of her death,' I asked.

'We did. He said he was in London, reading scripts at his flat. Alone. He won't say anything else without his solicitor present. I'd love to nail him for that job, you know. I'm sure as hell he's guilty.'

'But what a way to return to the scene of a crime, sir, to bring another woman and have a go at her ...'

'Exactly, young Nick. Exactly what I thought. By doing it like that, no one would suspect his part in the first crime, would they? Except experienced CID men ... What a clever sod, what a cunning bastard he really is ... How he can come over in such a charming way on screen beats me, it really does ...'

'So what are you going to do now, sir?'

'Wait,' he said. 'Wait with my eyes open and with that file never closed.'

And that file is still open.

Chapter 10

A brief reflection
solves the mystery.
BISHOP WILLIAM STUBBS (1825-19001)

AS I MENTIONED EARLIER in this book, I'm sure most young constables have ambitions to arrest a suspected murderer. Certainly, many fostered this dream when I joined the service, so when I started work within the CID, I looked forward to such an occasion.

I knew that if another murder was reported, I would be drafted onto the enquiry as a member of a team. For those purposes, a team comprises two detectives. They are either two detective constables or a detective sergeant with a detective constable. They are based at the incident room, which is an office established for the duration of the investigation. Each team is allocated specific tasks which are called 'actions', and in this way each team investigates a particular aspect of the crime until that aspect has been totally exhausted and, if possible, clarified. The outcome of this action is made known to those in charge of the incident room, so that the result can be filed and recorded. The result of one team's enquiries may have relevance to another action being dealt with by another team – collation of such links is the work of the clerical staff within the incident room.

The incident room can be established in a police

station, perhaps by using a recreation room or even a games room – anything will suffice so long as it is large enough to accommodate all the stationery and paraphernalia of a big investigation, in addition to some forty or more detectives working in teams of two. In remote situations, the incident room may even be based in a village hall, community centre, schoolroom or any other suitable accommodation. A detective sergeant runs the administrative side of the work in this room, while overall charge of the work of the incident room, and allocation of actions, is in the hands of an experienced detective inspector or chief inspector. In charge of the overall enquiry will be a detective superintendent or perhaps a detective chief superintendent, depending upon the size of the police force involved or, of course, the nature of the investigation.

I knew that all detectives felt the thrill of the chase when instructed to attend a briefing following the report of a murder; it meant working a twelve-hour day, usually from 9 a.m. until 9 p.m., until the killer was caught or the enquiry ended. But the camaraderie and excitement of this vital aspect of crime investigation are never exhausted, even in the most experienced of detectives. And, fortunately for the expansion of my police experience, albeit with the utmost sympathy for the victim, we did receive a report of a murder whilst I was an Aide.

It came at 8.45 a.m. one Monday morning, just as we were all arriving for the day's work. PC John Rogers took the call.

I heard him say, 'Just a moment, Mr Flint. I think you ought to speak to the CID.'

Detective Sergeant Gerry Connolly heard this interchange, nodded his understanding of its nature and went through to his office to take the call. He came back a few seconds later and said to us, 'I think we've got a murder on our hands, lads. I'm going round to have a look – No. 16 Driffield Terrace. Nick, you come with me. John, send a car round to that address, will you? With a uniformed man to seal off the house. Tell him to liaise with me there. Don't do anything further until you hear from me, and don't tell the press, not at this stage. And John, call the doctor; ask him to meet me there urgently.'

He asked me to go with him because I happened to be the only other CID man present on duty; Paul Wharton was working a late shift, and it was Ian Shackleton's day off. On the way to the house, which was a five-minute drive, Gerry told me that the first thing was to examine the body without touching it and without touching anything else in the house. The doctor would be required to certify death, however, and as the local police doctor, he would be advised on the need to touch as little as possible and not to move the body. It was vital that the scene of a murder be interfered with as little as possible.

We arrived to find a youth standing in the doorway of the terrace cottage. He looked pale and ghastly, and I guessed he was suffering from shock. He came to meet us, recognizing Connolly.

'In there,' he said, almost sobbing the words. 'In the kitchen ...'

'You're Mr Flint, are you?' asked Connolly.

'Yes, I'm ...'

'Wait here,' Gerry said to the youth. 'Nick, follow me and don't touch a thing; in fact, put your hands in your pockets.'

The front door led directly off the street into a narrow passage, and I noticed a *Daily Mail* stuck in the letter-box. Inside, I was tempted to pull it from the letter-box but resisted in time. I could see the date – it was that morning's edition. Inside, the stairs ascended to the left while the passage continued through the building. On the right was the front room, with a door opening into it from that passage; further along was a dining-room, also with the door standing open. The passage was carpeted with a long, dark maroon runner and bore one or two pictures along its walls; there was a mirror, too, and a small stand for walking-sticks.

At the end of the passage was the kitchen. This was at the back of the house, and as I peered beyond Gerry's bulky shape, I could see the legs of an elderly lady who lay on the floor.

'I'll have to go in,' he said gently. 'You stand at the door and look into the kitchen; keep your hands in your pockets and just look around. Note things in your memory, the position of everyday things … Has she washed up? Used the kitchen table? Had a meal? Is there anything odd about the scene?'

As Gerry entered the kitchen with all the caution of his years in CID work, I stood and watched. The dead lady was in her nightdress and was laid with her head touching the outer door and her neck at an awkward angle, twisted savagely to the left. Blood covered the tiled floor in the region of her head; it was dark and congealed. She wore slippers but her legs were bare and her hair was covered with an old-fashioned hair-net. Gerry stood at her side, mentally noting a hundred and one tiny details before he carefully leaned forward to touch her forehead.

'Cold as ice,' he said gently. 'She's dead all right, been dead a while by the look of it.'

As he visually examined the body, I looked around

the kitchen. The window over the sink was broken, and I could see slivers of glass in the sink. The catch was unfastened and the window, of the transom type, was open, but not wide enough to admit the average-sized person. I saw a torch on the floor too, not far from her right hand, and her walking-stick lay under the table. The table was set for breakfast with a packet of cornflakes and a bowl, a jar of marmalade and some butter, with a sugar bowl standing near a large mug.

On the mantelpiece, a tea caddy was standing with its lid off, and a corner cupboard had its door standing wide open, with the lids off several tins and jars.

'What do you make of it, Nick?' Gerry turned to me, not moving from his position.

'It looks as though somebody's broken in during the night, Sergeant. The glass in the sink shows the window was smashed from the outside. The villain opens it and climbs in through that window – it's large enough, then he closes it slightly once he's in. He begins looking for money, I think – all those lids off jars – and she hears him. She's in bed but gets her torch, comes downstairs, collects a walking-stick on the way, possibly from that stand in the passage, and comes in here to investigate. She's a brave lady. He goes for her – hits her with something, or she falls and smashes her head against the door or something else. A forensic pathologist will help determine that. And having done the foul deed, chummy leaves, by either the front door or the kitchen door.'

'Not the kitchen door, Nick. She's lying against it. It wouldn't open, so he couldn't leave that way. It would be the front door, then. Is the key in?'

I went to have a look. It was hanging on a string behind the letter-box. So many people made their keys available in this trusting manner, but with only one key to a household's front door, this was often the only convenient method of letting more than one person use it.

I then wondered if this lady lived alone, or whether she had a family, or even lodgers. That would have to be established very soon.

Gerry Connolly was saying, 'That seems to be the sequence of events, but we've a lot of work to do before we can definitely establish that. Now, we need our scenes-of-crime men, official photographer, two uniform constables to seal the rear and front entrances to everyone except investigators. The doctor's been called. I'll have to inform the D/C/I, get the official wheels in motion. And now what, Nick?'

I was puzzled for a moment, but recovered to say, 'Interview that youth, Mr Flint. It seems he found her.'

'Right, that's vital – and Nick, always remember that the person who finds the body, or the person who was last to see the victim alive, is the prime suspect. Lots of killers seem to think suspicion is removed from them if they report finding the body. Never forget that likelihood. So I will interview Mr Flint, but you can sit in; it'll be good experience.'

'Thanks, Sarge.'

'And what else must we do immediately?'

I thought we had covered most of the immediate actions, and he smiled.

'We need to search the house, Nick, in case the killer's still here, hiding, sleeping off a drunken stupor … villains do that, you know. And don't forget there could be another body in the house …'

Together, without touching the areas that might bear fingerprints, we searched every room, every wardrobe, cupboard and hiding place, under beds, in the toilet, in the loft and then outside in the coalhouse and outside loo. No one was hiding there, and there was not another dead body in the house.

'Won't be a moment, Mr Flint,' Gerry called as he caught sight of the anxious youth who was still waiting outside. 'We'll have a word with you in a second.'

Using the official radio in his car, he called the office and said, 'It's a murder investigation; address 16 Driffield Terrace, Eltering. Elderly lady found dead in suspicious circumstances after the house has been broken into. Please notify all departments and ask them to liaise with me at the scene. Call D/S Barber and ask him to establish an incident room; we can use the billiard room at Eltering nick. And I want immediate house-to-house enquiries – get Barber to recruit some teams straight away.'

In the force control room, there was a pre-arranged list of experts who had to be called to the scene of a suspected murder, and they would now be summoned. An incident room would be established and the whole drama surrounding a murder would now be set in motion.

Dr Stamford, who served as police doctor for Eltering, arrived and was shown the body. He was prepared to certify death but not the cause; that would be determined later that day by a post-mortem examination.

'Right,' said Connolly when Dr Stamford had gone. 'We'll talk to that man Flint now, Nick. Let's get him seen and on his way before the cavalry arrive.'

This meant an interview about the circumstances of his discovery of the body, followed by a written statement from him in which all the essential points were incorporated. That would be filed in a statement file, and all the relevant facts extracted for inclusion in a file index system. No detail was too insignificant in such an enquiry, and the interrogation of any witness would inevitably be dramatic for them, sometimes giving them the feeling that they were under suspicion. If they could not appreciate the lengths to which the police had to go to catch a murderer, then it was unfortunate.

Sitting in the front passenger seat of the CID car, with me in the rear, Connolly interviewed Nigel Flint. He was twenty-two years old and lived alone in a flat at No. 14A Market House, Market Place, Eltering. He was a clerk with a large-scale haulage contractor who operated from spacious premises on the outskirts of Eltering. He told us that the dead lady was Miss Edith Holt, who was in her seventies, and said he would be prepared to make the formal identification.

'I know, er, knew, her as Aunty Edie,' he told us. 'She was a close friend of my mother's. My mother lives on that new estate off Strensford Road, St Hilda's Way, Number 3. Anyway, she isn't a real aunt, she's not related to us, Mr Connolly, but ever since I was tiny, I've called her Aunt Edie.'

'That establishes your links with her,' said Connolly. 'So tell us about finding her this morning.'

I could see that this was going to be a traumatic time for Flint, but he took a deep breath and said, 'I always pop in to see her on my way to work. Every morning. Mum asked me to do it, to see if Aunt Edie wanted anything. Groceries, rent paid, bits and pieces for the house. Last week, she was on about getting a new toaster, that sort of thing.'

'So you called this morning. What time?'

'Just before quarter to nine. Twenty to, or thereabouts.'

'And what did you find?'

'Well, the first thing was the paper. It was still in the letter-box, so I thought she must still be in bed. She did lie in late sometimes.'

'Was the door shut?'

'Yes, closed, but not locked. I tried it. I don't have a key, but she leaves one on a string behind the letter-box, so I can let myself in if I have to. Anyway, it was open, Mr Connolly, which I thought was funny, seeing the paper was still there. When I got inside, I shouted upstairs but there was no reply, so I went through to the kitchen ... she always had her breakfast in the kitchen ... and, well, there she was.'

'You didn't see her before you got to the kitchen?'

Flint was puzzled at this, so Connolly elaborated.

'Was the kitchen door closed or open as you approached it?'

'Oh, closed – well, not latched, if you know what I mean. Closed almost completely. I hadn't to turn the handle to open it, I just pushed it open and ... saw her.'

'Look, Nigel, I know this is painful, but what exactly did you do next?'

'I could see she was dead, all that blood ... I just ran out and called you from the kiosk.'

'Which kiosk?'

'At the end of this street, on the corner.'

'Did you touch her? Speak to her? Look upstairs to see if there was an intruder about? Anything like that?'

'No, nothing. I just panicked and ran.'

Having recorded Nigel Flint's account, Gerry let him go; he had the awesome task of informing his own mother of this because, until now, he had not spoken to anyone save ourselves. But already a crowd of interested onlookers was gathering outside Edith Holt's little home, and by this time the cavalry – the mass of police and scientific investigators – was beginning to assemble.

'Right, Nick, you go back to the office and join the staff of the incident room. A typist will be allocated, so get her to type up this statement and distribute copies to all key personnel. Make sure the D/C/I gets one. We'll need to interview Flint again, I'm sure, about Aunt Edie's life-style, whether she encouraged visitors or whether she was rumoured to have money around the house, that sort of thing.'

I nodded my understanding as he went on, 'And make a statement yourself, get it typed up and entered into the system. Detail the facts you noticed in the house – the *Daily Mail*, the state of the kitchen, the window and so on.'

When I returned to Eltering Police Station, it was almost eleven o'clock and a detective inspector, detective sergeant and detective constable had already arrived in a large van from Headquarters to begin the setting-up of the incident room. Two GPO engineers were installing outside lines for the public to use, and Barbara, a strikingly beautiful typist, had been drafted in. The CID had brought a massive box of stationery, statement forms, pens and pencils and all the requirements of an office. They had produced a blackboard, two typewriters, a photocopying machine, a duplicating machine and even a couple of desks. I introduced myself and they gave me a statement form so that I could begin to compile my own statement. Barbara was already installed at a desk and had boiled a kettle, also brought by the CID, along with coffee, tea and two bottles of milk. Teams of detectives from all over the county had been drafted in, and they had been instructed to report at Eltering for the first conference at 2 p.m.

As this was happening, the body was being

photographed, as was the house and especially the kitchen and its broken window; fingerprint experts were examining the house too, and a forensic scientist was studying the corpse in its position before moving it to a mortuary for a post-mortem. The coroner had been informed, and the press had now heard of the death and were clamouring for news.

The next two or three hours were a whirlwind of activity, and I found myself heavily involved in helping to set up the incident room. Having been to the house and seen the body, I wrote the facts on the blackboard so that all the incoming CID officers could see it. It said: 8.45 a.m., Monday, 18 April. Body of Miss Edith Holt, 72 years, spinster, found at No. 16 Driffield Terrace. 5'4" tall, slim build, grey hair with hairnet, blue eyes. Dressed in white nightdress and pink slippers, and found lying in kitchen. Death believed from a head wound. Intruder had entered via kitchen window by breaking in; not known if anything stolen. Scene visited by doctor, forensic pathologist, SOCO, photographers, detective superintendent and assistant chief constable.' (In fact, the ACC had travelled all the way from Northallerton to pay his visit.) The notes on the blackboard also included Nigel Flint's name and address, and a brief physical description of him. As he was the finder of the body, we needed to know if other residents had seen him entering or leaving the house, or whether someone of a different description had been observed.

'Nick,' said Connolly a few minutes before two o'clock, 'pop round to the murder house in the car, see if any of our lads are still there; if so, tell 'em to get themselves round here to the CID conference. It starts at 2 p.m.'

I drove round to Miss Holt's house, now the scene of

immense public interest, and the constable on duty recognised me and allowed me inside. The front door was closed to prevent peeping in by ghouls; ghouls always gather at the scene of a dramatic death, a fire, traffic accident, air crash and similar event. I went to the kitchen where the scenes-of-crime officers were still working and told them of the conference; one would attend while the other two worked. The volunteer said he would come back with me in the car. The body had now been removed, and there was no one else in the house.

On the way out, I halted, for I had noticed a trilby hat hanging behind the front door. It looked fairly new. With the door standing open, it had not been noticed, and I could not recall seeing it that morning when I had noticed the *Daily Mail*. But I could not say for sure whether or not it had been there, for the door had been standing open all the time I had been in the house on that first occasion.

'That hat,' I said to my SOCO companion. 'It's odd, eh? In a spinster's home ...'

'We'll need to have it identified,' he said with no more ado. 'Find out whom it belongs to, how it came to be here. We can trace its sale through the manufacturer, and you might even trace the buyer through its retail outlet.' He lifted the grey felt trilby from the hook at the back of the door, popped it into a large plastic bag and labelled it as an exhibit. We took it back to the incident room.

The first conference was conducted by Connolly, who outlined the facts. He read out Flint's statement, and then mine, and said that the preliminary opinion of the pathologist was that Miss Holt had died from several blows to the head with a blunt instrument of some kind. That afternoon's post-mortem would confirm or refute that, but no murder weapon had been found. The assembled detectives, thirty in all, were divided into teams of two, and each team was given a specific action. Many were already involved in house-to-house enquiries in the area; one 'action' was to find out Miss Holt's financial position, another was to interview night people, such as bakers, other policemen, early-morning travellers in lorries that passed through, to see if anyone had been seen in suspicious circumstances. Another team had to make discreet enquiries into the background and character of Nigel Flint.

I then mentioned the trilby hat.

'Right, Nick. Action for you. Trace the owner. Right?'

'Right,' I said.

And so the murder investigation got underway.

I began my action by noting the manufacturer's name and address from the label inside the hatband; the hat was size 6½, and it was in almost new condition. The scenes-of-crime people took a photograph of it, but the felt texture would not reveal any fingerprints. I found it had been made in Bradford, and so I rang the CID of Bradford City Police and asked them to visit the factory to determine its history since manufacture. This could be done by a code number I discovered inside the leather headband.

'I'm going to ask Flint if he saw it this morning,' I told Gerry Connolly. 'It might belong to somebody who called regularly on the old lady.'

'Good idea,' he said. I went to his home address, but there was no reply, so I went to the office where he worked. He was at his desk, pale and quiet, and the manager had no objection to my speaking with him. I showed him the trilby, still in its plastic bag.

'It was hanging behind the front door,' I explained. 'Do you know if it belongs to any of your aunt's visitors?'

'Are you saying the killer left it behind?' he asked.

'It's possible,' I said. 'I'm trying to find out more about it – who put it there, for example, whether it was there when you went in this morning.'

He thought hard and then said, 'Yes, it was there. It doesn't belong to her and I've never seen a friend wearing it. When I walked in, I pushed the door open, but the draught blowing from the kitchen blew it shut. When I ran out to phone, I had to open that door – and I saw the hat ... it didn't mean anything then, Mr Rhea, but, well, is it the killer's?'

'Let's say it might lead us to a suspect,' I said. I got him to make a written statement confirming the presence of that hat and he signed it, asking, 'But can you honestly find out who it belongs to?'

'It won't be easy,' I admitted. 'In fact, it might be impossible, but we'll do our best.'

'They say every murderer leaves a clue behind,' he said.

'It's often the case,' I agreed, leaving him to his work.

When I returned to the incident room, Connolly hailed me.

'Ah, Nick, old son. Just the chap. That bloody trilby of yours. We've found the owner – or rather he's found us.'

'Oh?' This sounded interesting.

'It belongs to the assistant chief,' he laughed. 'He came to visit the scene of the crime at lunch-time and, being the gentleman he is, he took his hat off and hung it behind the door. Then he forgot it! It's his, Nick, so cancel that action. If that had been any of us doing such a daft thing, we'd have been bollocked up hill and down dale!'

I looked at the hat in my hand, and I remembered the words of Nigel Flint.

'Sergeant,' I said, 'I think Nigel Flint is our killer. He's just stated to me that he saw this hat behind the door this morning, when he found Edith dead. He can't have, because it wasn't there then. He's lying. Is he trying to throw suspicion onto the owner of the hat?'

'I think we'd better have another word with Nigel Flint,' he said.

I did not go to that interview, for it required the skills of a very experienced detective, and so Gerry Connolly went to see Nigel once more.

Nigel admitted killing her. Desperately short of cash, he knew Aunt Edith had cash hidden all over the house and had broken in to steal some of it, intending to make it look like a burglary. He'd broken in during the night hours, around two o'clock in the morning, but she had caught him – in his panic to avoid discovery, he'd picked up the electric iron which had been on the draining-board and had repeatedly struck her with it. She never knew it was him, he was sure, and that gave him some relief, but he had run off, taking the iron with him. He'd thrown it in the river to get rid of it. He wept as he gave his statement to Gerry Connolly, saying over and over again that he'd had no intention of killing Aunt Edie …

We recovered the iron from the river, and the forensic experts found strands of her hair and blood upon it. I did not arrest or charge Nigel with his crime – that was done by Sergeant Connolly, but I did feel I had done my bit towards arresting a killer. He pleaded guilty to burglary but not guilty to the charge of murder. The court accepted a plea of guilty to manslaughter, however, and he was given five years imprisonment for the manslaughter, and two for the burglary, the sentences to run concurrently. He'd stolen £23 from her house.

He is now out of prison and living in Lancashire.

Another case remains a puzzle, at least in my mind if not in the official records.

One December morning, when drizzle and fog made the countryside damp and miserable, a farmer's wife called Irene Sheldon came into the police station. She reported that her husband, William, was missing from home. He was seventy-two years old and rather frail, and she was worried about him.

Ian Shackleton interviewed her. She was a very attractive woman, well dressed in green clothes which highlighted her long auburn hair and her pale skin. There was an aura of power about her, the sort of woman who was dominant and capable, the kind who could run any successful business, ranging from a farm to a restaurant. She was also capable of undertaking manual tasks about the farm, shearing the sheep or loading bales of hay, although she usually got others to perform such labouring tasks.

'So why would he go missing?' Ian asked her.

She hung her handsome head. 'He found out I was having an *affaire*,' she readily admitted. 'I've been seeing another man – but that's not a criminal offence, is it?' She stuck out her chin defiantly.

'You are much younger than him?' commented Ian.

'Yes, I'm forty-five. I'm his second wife. His first died eight years ago, and I used to be his housekeeper. He married me five years ago. He's too old. There's too much of an age-gap between us. I should have known better, really, but he is a charming old man, really charming ...'

'So what precisely prompted him to run off?'

'We had a row. He found out I was seeing Bernard – my feller – at weekends and evenings. We'd been away, you see, me and Bernard, to the Royal Show and to other events. I mean, I do need a younger man ...'

'This row,' Ian quizzed her, 'was it violent?'

She shook her head. 'No, he's not a violent man, not at all. He sometimes sulks a lot, gets very depressed and moody, and when I said I could not stop seeing Bernard, well, he just went absolutely quiet. That was last night. He went to bed early, soon after nine, and was very quiet. When I took him his tea up this morning, his bed was empty. We slept in separate rooms, by the way, His outdoor clothes have gone, the ones he works in, but he's taken no money or anything. His car's still there.'

'Shotguns? Has he taken any guns? Gone shooting maybe?'

'No, I looked. The gun's still there, the one he uses for rabbiting.'

'Was he suicidal at all, during the time you've known him?'

'Yes, often,' she said. 'He can be very jealous; if he took me to the hunt ball and I was asked by someone else to dance, he would go into a huff and sulk all night. Several times, he's threatened to end it all because he thought I'd stopped loving him. He's odd, like that, very dark at times, very moody and deep.'

'Normally, when an adult goes missing, we are not too interested,' said Ian. 'Adults are free to leave home whenever they wish. So unless there is a suggestion of a crime either by them, or against them, we take little action. But I think in this case there is real concern for his safety. We'll circulate details and a description of him.'

'What about a search? Don't you make a search?' she asked.

'Not unless we have good cause, and at this stage there is no cause for a search – besides, where do we start? No, we will circulate the surrounding police officers in the hope they might find him wandering or that he is seen somewhere so that we have an indication of his whereabouts. Old folks do wander, you know. They get on buses, go for long walks, ride bikes, spend time in pubs and cafés ...'

Ian talked to her for a long time, eliciting from her what amounted to a most frank confession of her *affaires* with other men, the current one being Bernard Balcombe, who was a salesman for cattle feeds. Some she had managed to conceal from poor old William, but this one had come to a head in this terrible manner. Ian asked if there was a likelihood that William had known of the previous ones, even if he had not said so. She thought it was possible, but unlikely. He also learned that, by his first wife, William had two sons, and so Ian said he would ask them if they had seen their father. She gave us their addresses, thanked us for our interest and left.

'What do you make of her?' Ian asked when she had gone.

'She comes over as a cold and calculating woman,' I said. '"Chilling" is the word I'd use.'

'The sort who would drive a fellow to suicide to get her hands on his money, eh?' He floated his thoughts in this way.

'I wouldn't put it past her.' My own views were that she was a calculating sort of woman.

'I'm off for a word with his sons,' he decided.

204

He returned two hours later. The old man had not gone to either of his sons during his anguish, something they both found odd. Each said that in the past old William had gone to one or other of his sons to complain about his new wife: that she was getting through too much money, that she was not caring for him, that she was spending time away from the farm, meeting other men ...

'So he did know she was being unfaithful, long before this *affaire*.'

'Yes, he knew, all right. He was moody, they both agreed with that, but he was never suicidal. They think he might have gone for a long walk, to think things over. But they will ask around their relatives and go out and look for him. They know his haunts.'

'Is the farm his own?' I asked.

'Yes, he owns it outright; it's worth a fortune. He's changed his will, by the way, only in the last month; Irene does not know he's done that.'

'So who benefits?' I wondered.

'The farm and all the stock are willed to both lads. He's cut her out completely; he reckons if she goes with other men now, she can find some other mug to look after her in old age. He's had enough of her.'

'So Irene thinks she will get the farm if he dies, eh?' I asked Ian.

'So the sons tell me.'

We heard nothing of William Sheldon for the next two days, in spite of searches by his wife, his sons and friends of the family and in spite of our own wide circulation. Then we got a 999 call from a fisherman.

'There's a body in the beck,' he said. 'The River Elter, about a mile downstream from Warren Bridge. It looks like a man.'

I went with the uniformed police constable, and we drove to the area known as Warren Ings. It lay some three miles from the town centre, and the River Elter wove a deep and winding course through the flat countryside. For well over two miles, the river skirted Sheldon's land, where it formed a formidable barrier to the south of the extensive farm, I guided the constable to Warren Bridge, where we found the fisherman waiting for us.

'It's a fair walk down here.' He showed us a footpath along the edge of the river, and we followed him through the hazels and alders that lined the banks.

We came eventually to a long, wide curve in the river where, on the bank which formed the outer rim of that curve, there were many thick alder trees whose roots formed a curious array of stems which protruded from the water. The flow of the river had gradually washed away the earth at this point, leaving the roots exposed, but the trees had not been weakened by it. They grew as strong and as firm as ever.

'In that pool,' said the fisherman, whose name we had learned was Frederick Shearman and who lived at Thirsk. He indicated a deep pool at the far side of those alders, and we approached to see the distinctive shape of a body submerged in the clear water. It looked very deep here, and the body was below the surface, being washed gently by the movement of the flow on this wide curve.

I studied its position for a few moments, noting that the bank over the position of the body was high and sheer. It was sandy in appearance, and there were sand martins' nest holes at intervals along the miniature cliff. It was about six or seven feet high, with a sheer drop into the water. A tangle of alder roots was some six or seven feet upstream, but directly below the sheer bank the

206

water looked very deep indeed. I asked the constable to go and radio for assistance; I needed to have the attendance of Gerry Connolly and the police underwater search unit, whose task would be to recover the corpse. In addition, I needed the inevitable doctor to certify death.

There was no need for heroics at this late stage. No one dived in to effect a dramatic rescue, for that this person was dead was never in doubt. As we waited for the next stage of this development, I wondered if I was looking at the remains of poor old William Sheldon.

With the eventual arrival of our experts, the body was recovered but, as it came out of the water with the aid of two police frogmen, there was a shock for us all. A cement block had been tied to its neck on the end of a length of rope, and that had kept the body anchored to the bottom of the river.

The body was that of William Sheldon; his eldest son, Stanley, later had the unpleasant job of making a formal identification of the remains. The post-mortem revealed that death had been due to drowning, which meant he was alive when he had entered the water, and there was a large abrasion to the back of his head. The pathologist could not say what had produced that – it might have been caused by the cement block striking him as it dragged him down, or contact with rocks under the surface, or he might have been knocked unconscious before entering the water.

At the inquest which followed, the coroner asked the pathologist the questions that we had all been asking ourselves and which, indeed, we had also put to him.

'Doctor,' he said, 'tell me this. In your expert opinion, could Mr Sheldon have committed suicide? Could he have walked to the banks of that river, tied the block around his own neck and then jumped in, to be weighted down until he drowned?'

'Yes, sir, he could. He was a frail man but, being a farmer, he could easily have carried that block. It is one of many that are still around the farm buildings. He used them for securing stack sheets against high winds.'

'So a determined man could have committed suicide in this way?'

'Yes, sir.'

'Now, tell me, Doctor. The abrasion on his skull. Was that sufficient to render him unconscious?'

'Yes, in my opinion it was.'

'And can you say whether that was inflicted before or after he entered the water?'

'I can say it was inflicted when he was alive, sir, and we know he was alive when he entered the water. It is possible that someone knocked him unconscious with a heavy blow to the head, tied the weight around his neck and threw him into the river. That is not impossible but I cannot state with any certainty that that is what actually happened. We can only speculate upon what actually occurred, and I cannot speculate further upon the available evidence.'

'But you can confirm that he died from drowning?'

'I can. If he had been dead when he entered the water, there would not have been water in his lungs. I have tested the water found in his lungs and confirm it is the same as that which flows in the River Elter.'

'And that is significant?' asked the coroner.

The pathologist continued: 'Yes, sir. This means he was not drowned elsewhere and brought here for disposal. I confirm that he died from drowning, sir. But whether he was thrown in or threw himself in is something I cannot say. Nor can I say whether or not he was conscious when he entered the river.'

Having listened to this evidence, the coroner summed up.

'We are told by the second Mrs Sheldon that her husband was suicidal, but no note has been found; we are also told by his sons that, although he was moody and upset at his wife's self-confessed unfaithfulness, he was not suicidal. So there is a conflict of evidence here. However, I must place on record that his body was found in the River Elter and that he was alive when he entered the water, in a state of either consciousness or unconsciousness. His death is due to drowning, and there was an abrasion on his head which was sufficient to render him unconscious. I am not prepared to accept that William Sheldon took his own life; there is no evidence of that. Nor can I speculate under what precise circumstances his body came to be in the river – it is possible that a third party or parties knocked him unconscious and threw him into the river, his head weighted down so that he drowned. I therefore record an open verdict.'

This caused a buzz of interest in the court, for such a verdict was rather unusual, and the following day's newspapers bore headlines such as 'Mystery of Farmer's Final Hours'.

Mrs Sheldon, with enormous suspicion hanging over her, left the farm to live in Wales, and the two sons moved back. Bernard Balcombe also moved on, having taken a job with another animal feeds firm in the Midlands.

So the facts surrounding the death of William Sheldon remain a mystery, and it was only three weeks after the inquest that I came to the end of my period as an Aide to CID. I left with happy memories and with this puzzle in my mind. Even now I still ponder over William's death, wondering whether it was murder or suicide.

We shall never know until someone confesses.

That case was the last in which I was involved as a Constable in Disguise. I wondered if, over those interesting months, I had sufficiently impressed those faceless Powers-that-Be who decide the progress of one's career and whether, at some distant time, I would join the CID. Gerry Connolly did say I'd fulfilled his expectations and that he hoped one day I would be selected for a detective training course as a prelude to joining the CID. But I knew that such a transfer could not be immediate – even if I had been successful in my recent work, I would have to await a vacancy and there were many ambitious young officers queueing for very few CID posts.

In the meantime, I returned to my beat at Aidensfield, there to continue my work as a rural constable in the stunning countryside of North Yorkshire.

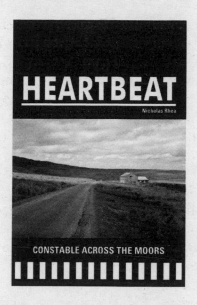

Police Constable Nick Rhea continues his heart-warming account of rural bobbying on the North Yorkshire moors and finds himself dealing with a host of intriguing characters who live and work on the wild moors.

In his latest adventures he investigates a case of witchcraft, which local lass Katherine Hardwick employs to rid herself of a troublesome suitor.

Then there's the strange story of the insurance man who covers a dog against its persistent theft, and unscrupulous love-making.

ISBN 9781906373375
Price £7.99

Constable By The Sea

During a seasonal break from his usual village beat on the North Yorkshire moors, young Police Constable Nick Rhea finds himself involved with holiday-makers and their problems.

As well as his normal seaside duties, how does he cope with a man who has lost his false teeth in the sea and another who wants to give away thousands of pounds, when drunk?

Then there's the stray Labrador that thinks he's a police dog and accompanies police officers on night patrols, and the anxious fisherman who daren't tell his wife that he owns a racehorse.

ISBN 9781906373399
Price £7.99

Constable On The Prowl

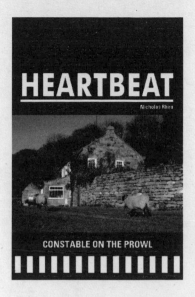

Young bobby Nick Rhea is settling into his new life patrolling the sleepy Aidensfield, but he still hates working nights.

Under the cover of darkness, Nick gets to know his colleagues. He also has his first encounter with local rogue Claude Jeremiah Greengrass, who is beating a hasty retreat from a lady's bedroom!

Practical jokes and friendship combine as Nick warms to life in the village he will soon *consider his home*.

ISBN 9781906373351
Price £7.99

Constable Along The Lane

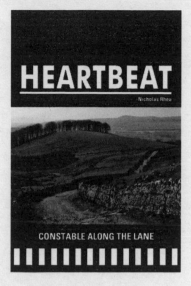

Crime comes to Aidensfield when haystacks are fired and Arnold Merryweather's ancient bus helps catch a car thief.

Rural bobby PC Nick Rhea gets more than he bargained for when he arrests a pig thief, and the pregnant pig, much to the annoyance of the police station cleaner!

But it's not all crime. A glider crashes into a thatched cottage and Nick also gets involved in a plot to force a Yorkshire miser to spend some money.

ISBN 9781906373405
Price £7.99

For more information about our books please visit
www.accentpress.co.uk